BETTER OFF DEAD
MOUNTAIN SHADOW MYSTERIES BOOK ONE

TARAH BENNER

ALSO BY TARAH BENNER

Witches of Mountain Shadow (Books 1-6)

Christmas in Mountain Shadow

The Witch's Fortune

Blood Ties

The Elven Blade

The Elderon Chronicles (Books 1-5)

The Lawless Saga (Books 1-4)

Bound in Blood

The Fringe (Books 1-5)

The Defectors Trilogy (Books 1-3)

Copyright © 2023 by Tarah Benner

All rights reserved.

This book is a work of fiction, and any similarities to any person, living or dead, are coincidental and not intentional.

No part of this book may be reproduced in any form or by any electronic or mechanical means, including information storage and retrieval systems, without written permission from the author, except for the use of brief quotations in a book review.

ISBN: 979-8392571239

www.tarahbenner.com

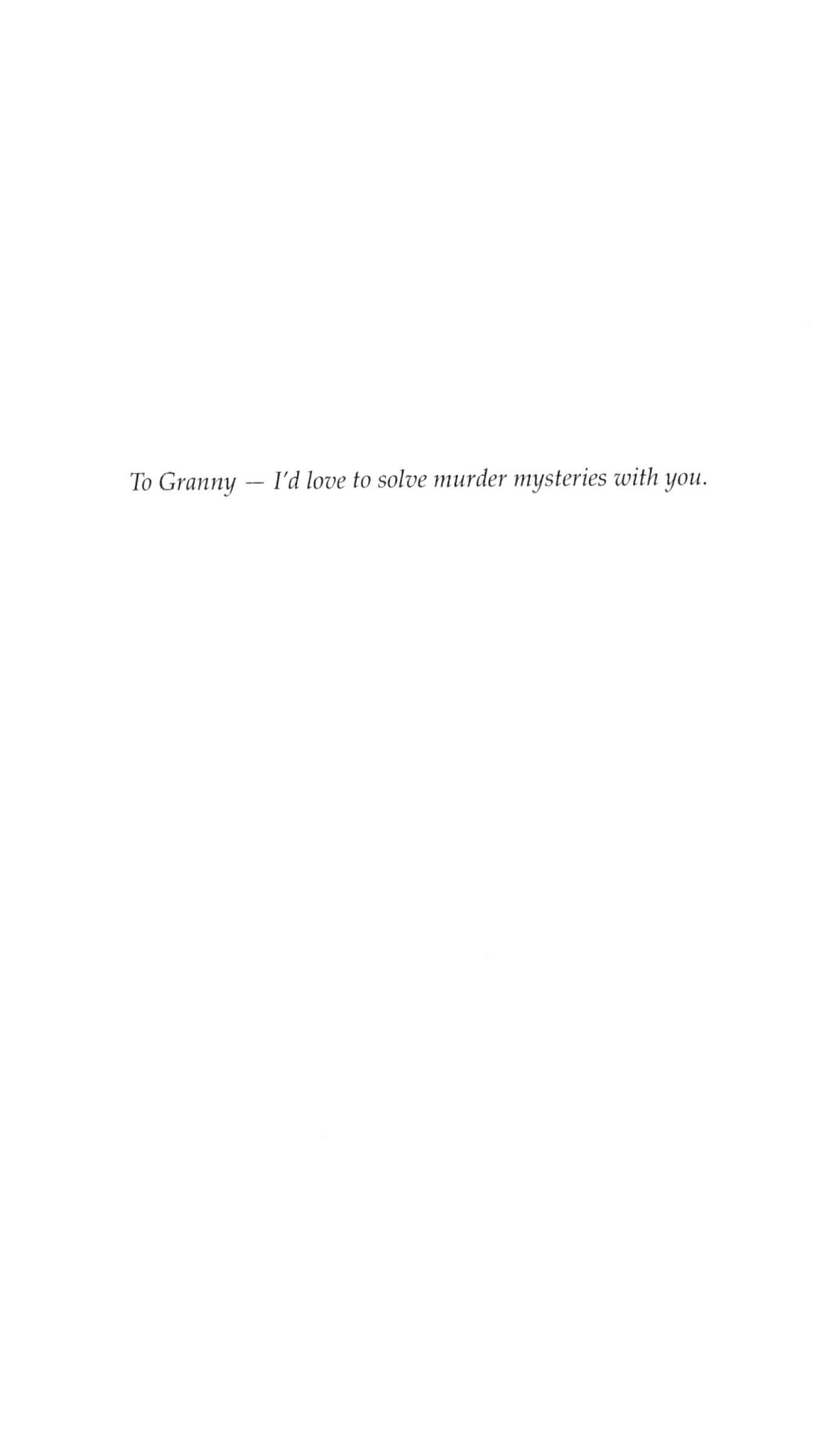

To Granny — I'd love to solve murder mysteries with you.

CHAPTER ONE

As I stared at the rat's nest of cables hanging from the wall, I realized that I'd been robbed. My brand-new smart TV was gone, leaving only the empty mount.

My tastefully decorated midcentury apartment looked like a war zone. Someone had knocked over my bird of paradise plant just inside the door and broken the white clay pot. Books and papers were strewn all over the living room floor, and one of my kitchen chairs had been upended.

My little home office in the corner was in complete disarray. They'd taken my fifteen-hundred-dollar desktop computer, as well as my laptop and iPad. Pens and highlighters were scattered all over my desk, along with the contents of my file sorter.

Moving in a daze, I went into the bedroom and stared at my mattress resting crookedly on the box spring — throw pillows lying pell-mell on the floor. The closet doors were wide open, as if someone had been rifling through my things, and the dresser drawers had been emptied.

I froze when I saw the jewelry box still sitting on my dresser. It didn't contain anything of value — just some inexpensive necklaces and rings that I wore on a regular basis. The family heirlooms were hidden in a shoebox under my bed, tucked between the Christmas decorations and a box of wool sweaters.

I knelt down and reached for the familiar battered box and froze when my hand skimmed the void between my twin plastic totes.

No. No, no, no, no, no.

Bending over, I pressed my temple all the way to the floor to confirm what I already knew. The box where I'd kept my most precious treasures was gone. Great-Grandma's pearls, Gramps's silver watch, my dad's class ring — all of it was gone.

I sat up and tried to breathe as a hard lump formed in my throat. What sort of thieves took a dusty old shoebox but left the antique black-walnut jewelry box that had been sitting out in plain sight?

The answer smacked me in the face almost immediately, but my brain kept searching for some other explanation.

There was only one person who knew what I'd kept in that shoebox, and I really, *really* didn't want it to be him.

My legs felt like jelly as I got to my feet and walked out into the living room. My heart was throbbing dully somewhere behind my collarbone as my gaze darted from the framed photo of the two of us resting crookedly on the end table to the cut-out picture of Todd's head that I'd pasted on a groom's body. The bobble-headed groom version of him dominated the center of my wedding dream board, along with a similar photo of me against a Hawaiian sunset.

With shaky hands, I dug my phone out of my back pocket and dialed my fiancé. Blood pounded in my ears, and the call went straight to voicemail.

Don't panic, I told myself. *It doesn't mean anything.*

Never mind that the manager at our wedding venue had called to let me know that our second-choice date was still available if we put down a deposit — the deposit that Todd was supposed to have dropped off *weeks* ago. I'd given him my half as soon as we'd decided on the venue, and he'd said he'd swing by on his way home the next day.

When Todd hadn't answered my call from work, I'd called the caterer, the bakery, the florist, and the DJ. None of them had received our deposits, either. I'd been spiraling the entire ride back to my apartment, preparing to confront Todd when he got home. And then I'd found . . . this.

It's not what you think, I told myself firmly. Todd couldn't have stolen the money.

I knew I'd sound like a crazy Bridezilla if I accused him, so I dialed the number for Southwest Airlines. I'd scribbled a confirmation number that Todd had given me in the corner of my wedding calendar, which was covered in a rainbow of sticky notes. Each color corresponded to a different aspect of the event, and I'd drawn a big pink heart around our date-iversary.

Todd had been strapped for cash after putting down the deposit on our venue, so I'd given him my credit card to purchase the plane tickets for our honeymoon in

Hawaii. My voice shook as I read off the confirmation number, hoping it was all a big misunderstanding.

We're sorry. We do not have a reservation that matches that number.

"Dammit." I hung up on the automated robot and tried Todd's number again.

This time, rather than his outgoing message, I got an automated reply: *The number you have dialed has been disconnected or is no longer in service.*

"No!" I yelled, jabbing my finger at the screen to end the call and chucking my phone onto the couch.

I stormed back into the bedroom, intent on throwing all his stuff onto the curb. But when I reached the dresser the two of us shared, I realized that the only drawers the "thieves" had bothered to empty had belonged to Todd. His clothes were gone, along with his laptop and charger. His half of the closet was also empty, and he'd taken one of my suitcases!

I couldn't believe it. Everything he'd ever said to me — all the plans we'd made — all of that was a lie. He hadn't worked as a delivery driver. Apparently, his job was conning gullible blondes out of their entire life savings and then ransacking their apartments for anything of value. Was his name even really *Todd*?

The thought made me want to be sick.

Just then, my phone buzzed from the living room, and I practically sprinted out of the bedroom to reach it in time. Part of me hoped that it was Todd calling to tell me that we'd been robbed — and that there was a ring of wedding scammers fleecing unsuspecting young couples all over Chicago.

"Hello?" I gasped.

"Caroline?" My mother's voice rang through the phone, and my heart dropped to my knees. "Are you all right?"

"Fine," I lied. "I just . . . had to run . . . to get the phone."

"Well, you really should sign up for a spin class or something. You sound as though you're about to have a cardiac event."

"What's up, Mom?" I asked. I wasn't in the mood.

"Why are you upset?"

"I'm not upset," I gritted, wishing I'd thought to check the caller ID. "I'm just . . . dealing with some stuff right now."

"Planning a wedding is always stressful — particularly when it's thrown together so *hastily.*" Mom's voice ratcheted up to her judgmental octave on the last word, and I rolled my eyes so hard I thought I might pull a muscle.

"Uh-huh."

I couldn't bring myself to explain that the wedding was off — and that the guy I'd introduced her to was a fraud. I *certainly* couldn't tell her he'd used my credit-card information to book his getaway flight and was probably halfway to Mexico by then.

"Well, I'm afraid I have some bad news . . ."

My stomach did a nasty flop as my mind flew to the worst-case scenario. Had Todd somehow roped my mom into his scheme and ripped her off, too?

"Your great-aunt Lucille — you know, Gran's sister?"

"I know who Aunt Lucille is, Mom."

"Yes, well, she passed away last night. The nursing

home just called to notify me, since your father was her next of kin. I guess she got a bad case of pneumonia and was too weak to fight it off."

"She *died*?"

"Yes. Poor thing."

I sank down on the edge of my ottoman, my chest constricting with a different sort of grief. It had been a few years since I'd seen Aunt Lucille, but I'd visited her plenty as a kid. She'd been an actress and a burlesque dancer in her day — the epitome of the lively, eccentric aunt. Lucille had never had any children of her own, so she'd doted on my dad.

"I'm sorry, honey. I know you were fond of her." Mom heaved a dramatic sigh. Given my current level of misery, I appreciated the effort to sound sincere. She and dad's side of the family had never been Hallmark-movie material. "But with your father gone and she and your grandmother on the outs . . ." Mom trailed off suggestively. "Maybe Lucille remembered you in her will?"

Ah, there it was. "That's really tacky, Mom."

"Don't bite my head off, Caroline! I was just stating the facts. I'm sorry to be the bearer of bad news. I just thought you'd like to know."

I pressed my lips together. Typical Mom. She always said what she was thinking, whether it was appropriate or not. It was this trait of hers that made Gran look as though she'd tasted something sour whenever the two of them were together.

"When's the funeral?" I asked, feeling suddenly very tired.

"You know I don't keep up with that side of the family.

You'll have to call your gran and ask. I've got to go, honey. I'm meeting the girls for drinks."

"Bye, Mom."

I was numb with sadness and rage as I hung up the phone and tossed it back onto the couch. I couldn't even absorb the fact that Aunt Lucille was gone. I was still reeling from Todd.

My fiancé wasn't my fiancé. This had all been one elaborate hoax. For the last six months, he'd been faking interest in me so that I'd fall in love with him — and it had worked.

That was the part that hurt the most.

But if that were true, I couldn't have been the only girl he'd done this to — certainly not the first. Todd had been the perfect boyfriend. Or, at least, he'd seemed perfect *for me*.

He would have had to, I thought darkly. Everything would have had to go exactly according to plan so that when he staged that romantic proposal at Garden of the Phoenix, I'd be so infatuated that I'd agree to marry him after knowing him for such a short time.

Wait. I looked down at my ring — the princess-cut diamond in a simple white-gold setting that I'd flaunted all over the office for weeks. If the engagement was a hoax, that meant I'd been showing off a fake diamond engagement ring!

I groaned aloud with embarrassment. Soon I'd have to tell my friends and everyone I worked with. It would be all anyone was gossiping about for months.

Suddenly my apartment felt much too small, and I had to grab hold of the low wall that divided my living room from the tiny kitchenette. A dull ringing had started in my ears, and I had the sudden feeling that I might pass out.

Fumbling for the latch on the sliding-glass door, I flung it wide open and stuck my head out into the muggy July heat. Cars and buses inched by four stories below, filling the air with the scent of exhaust. I could feel the humidity clinging to my skin and frizzing my hair, but the fresh air helped me think.

How long had Todd been planning this? Had he sought me out to swindle? Had he *targeted* me on the dating app I'd downloaded like some *Dateline* stalker?

How many other women had he proposed to? How many had he duped? Did he move from city to city working this scheme, or did he have multiple scams going at once?

A swoop of nausea accompanied that thought, and I staggered out onto the balcony and emptied the contents of my stomach. Thankfully, I'd been working nonstop on a new ad account at work and hadn't had time to eat lunch.

Wiping my mouth, I staggered inside. My gaze swiveled back to my wedding dream board — back to Todd's jovial face swimming in the cloud of peonies. I'd thought he'd looked so cute in that picture. Now all I could see was a liar.

My body seemed to move without consulting my brain, and my legs carried me across the room. Possessed by a rage I didn't know I could feel, I gripped the edges of the foam board and ripped it off my wall. It took a little of the paint with it, but that was the least of my problems.

Storming back onto the balcony, I howled into the void and chucked the whole thing over the railing. For a second, Todd's face and mine sort of drifted in the air before sinking to the ground like a rock.

As I watched it fall, I had a moment of panic that the foam board would land on a motorist's windshield and cause some terrible accident, but then my dream board hit the pavement and cracked neatly in two. I watched with grim satisfaction as a semi rolled by, crushing Todd's stupid face under twenty-four-inch wheels.

CHAPTER TWO

It had been five days since I'd learned that my fiancé was a fraud — five days since Todd had cleaned out my apartment and skipped town with all my money.

I was on my way to Gran's house in Colorado to help with Aunt Lucille's funeral arrangements. I'd flown from O'Hare to Denver the day before and then rented a car to drive the rest of the way to Mountain Shadow — a tiny town west of Colorado Springs.

Rain was coming down in droves as I navigated the winding mountain road. Huge rust-colored rock formations rose up on either side of the narrow highway, but I kept my gaze fixed straight ahead at the bleary set of taillights in front of me. Apparently July was monsoon season in Colorado, which meant regular rainstorms every afternoon.

The windshield wipers of my pitiful rental car were swiping frantically to keep up with the downpour, but it was still difficult to make out the road ahead. My stomach lurched each time the car scooted around one of the hairpin curves punctuated by jutting sandstone fins.

The last few days had been a mess. I'd had to cancel all my credit cards and change the locks on my doors, but there was no getting back the money I'd given Todd for our wedding.

According to the police, Todd Polinski had been an alias, and the account linked to his Venmo profile had already been drained of all funds. He'd likely booked himself a flight under another name and fled the country with all my money.

Even worse than being scammed by my fiancé was having to call everyone on our guest list to tell them that the wedding was off. After six or seven grueling phone calls, I'd drafted a lengthy email treatise and BCC'd the rest of our guests.

I hadn't had the guts to check my inbox since I'd left Chicago.

Replaying the early weeks Todd and I had spent together, I realized that there'd been signs. I'd just chosen to ignore them. Todd had never introduced me to any of his friends, but he was new to the city and didn't know many people. His parents had retired to Hawaii, he'd said, and he was an only child. I was supposed to meet his parents at the wedding.

He'd seemed just as excited to tie the knot as I was, and he'd taken an active role in planning our wedding. I hadn't thought twice about Venmoing him my half of the deposits so he could pay the vendors. I hadn't hesitated to give him my credit card so he could buy our plane tickets.

Looking back, I should have. I wasn't the kind of girl who got swept away by romance. I had a five-year plan and a 401(k) that I'd intended to fully fund by the time I was fifty. And I'd thrown it all away for him.

Todd was probably sipping Mai Tais on the beach with *our* honeymoon money, but his stealing from me didn't hurt nearly as much as my own naiveté. On our first date, Todd had told me he had dreams of becoming an actor, and I'd confessed that I secretly wanted to quit my job in marketing to write mystery novels. Apparently, he was *also* close with his ninetysomething-year-old grandmother and made a point to call her every day on his way home from work.

It was this last detail that really made me fall for him on that first date, but he'd probably spent hours snooping through my social-media profiles to figure out exactly what to say to me.

Over the last six months, we'd discovered all kinds of little things we had in common. We both loved Thai food and Colorado and old black-and-white movies. All those romantic coincidences that had seemed like destiny at the time now left a bitter taste in my mouth.

The sound of my own pathetic sobs echoed in the car, and I had to slow down to see the road through the haze of rain and tears. Squinting through the downpour, I spotted a brightly colored sign along the side of the road welcoming me to Mountain Shadow: *Experience the magic of the mountains.*

The highway dumped me out on Main Street, and I took a moment to get my bearings. I'd been to the little tourist town plenty of times as a kid, but the streets were still only vaguely familiar as I passed through downtown. The old brick buildings had been converted to shops, bars, restaurants, and apartments. I passed an old penny arcade, a fifties-style diner, an apothecary, a Christmas store, and a coffee shop called Déjà Brew.

At the thought of coffee, I got hit with an intense craving. I hadn't been sleeping well since the robbery and had subsisted mainly on coffee and non-dairy peanut-butter-fudge ice cream.

Gripped the steering wheel with an almost manic desperation, I whipped the little car around in a tight U-turn and zipped into an open spot. A neon purple sign with an all-seeing eye on a coffee cup beamed through the gloom as I hopped out into the rain and scurried toward the café.

A little bell over the door dinged as I came in, and the glorious scent of espresso, combined with the general coziness of the place, gave me an energizing lift. The shop was crowded with mismatched tables and chairs painted in various shades of purple. A bulletin board by the door was papered with festival posters and fliers for missing pets, and copies of *The Mountain Shadow Gazette* rested in a rack by the trash can.

I sighed. This place was just what I needed.

"Hey," came the lackadaisical greeting of the tattooed barista behind the counter.

She looked about my age — maybe twenty-eight or twenty-nine — but way, *way* cooler. She had stick-straight black hair pulled back in a careless ponytail, a nose ring, and a giant crystal hanging around her neck.

I managed something in the ballpark of "hello" and shuffled up to the register.

"What can I get — *oh*."

The barista's abrupt change in tone caught my attention, and I glanced down to check my reflection in the pastry case under the cash register.

The shirt I was wearing had a telltale stain from the jelly donut I'd inhaled on the drive. My shoulder-length blond curls were all frizzed-out from the rain, and I had cartoonish mascara tear tracks down both cheeks. To make matters worse, the stress of the sham wedding had been making my rosacea flare up, so my face looked extra red and puffy.

"Oh, god!" I hurriedly tried to scrub the mascara tracks from my cheeks, and the barista handed me a napkin.

"Rough day?"

"Rough *week*."

The barista bit her lip, taking in my whole situation with something like understanding in her golden-brown eyes.

"I just found out I was being swindled by my fiancé," I blurted, my throat getting tight the way it always did when I was about to cry. "He stole a bunch of money that was supposed to be for our wedding, robbed my apartment, and skipped town." I drew in a shaky breath and blew my nose on the rough paper napkin. "I'm pretty sure I'm not the first girl he's done this to."

"Are you serious?" The barista's eyes bugged out in a mixture of horror and fascination. It was the typical reaction to hearing any online-dating horror story, but I detected genuine sympathy in her voice. "Dude, I'm sorry. That *sucks*."

For some reason, it was this sweet stranger's earnest pity that *really* sent me over the edge. Big, fat tears leaked out of my eyes, and my nose immediately started to run. "I'm sorry," I hiccuped, dabbing under my nose and rubbing away the tears. "I don't know why I just told you all that."

"It's okay!" she said, reaching over the counter to give my wrist a squeeze.

I pulled a wan smile and dried the rest of my tears. I couldn't believe I'd just broken down in front of a random stranger. I glanced down at her name tag.

Amber — her name was Amber. So she wasn't a *total* stranger. That made this breakdown something of an improvement from the breakdown I'd had on the handyman who'd come to change out the locks, the customer-service lady from my bank, and the new client at work whose pitch meeting I'd totally bombed.

"Can I get a large mocha with oat milk and an extra shot?" I asked, trying to rein in the last of the waterworks.

"Girl, you don't need espresso. You need, like, the *opposite* of espresso."

A little rush of panic flared through me at the thought that my drug of choice might be withheld, and fresh tears welled up in my eyes.

"I'm *kidding*!" Amber cried, hurriedly patting my hand. "Oh, I'm sorry. Bad joke. I'm such an idiot. Girl, I've got you. Just one sec."

I sniffed and handed over my shiny new credit card. "Thanks."

Amber rang me up in two seconds flat and started making my latte with practiced efficiency. As I watched her pour the milk and tamp down the espresso, my phone buzzed for the hundred-millionth time. A deluge of notifications and reminders crowded my screen.

8:30 a.m. Submit revisions to slide deck
9:00 a.m. LuckyChow rebrand brainstorm

11:00 a.m. Team meeting
12:00 p.m. Lunch with Todd
2:30 p.m. Phone call with caterer

I also had no fewer than two hundred unread messages. Most of them were from friends and family I'd disinvited from the wedding. The rest were from clients and co-workers, though after my little breakdown at the pitch meeting, my supervisor had "suggested" that I take some time off and come back once I was "ready to play ball."

I knew what that meant. Either I came back focused, refreshed, and full of brilliant ideas, or I was out for good.

I sighed and shoved my phone back into my pocket. I needed to delete any wedding-related appointments. Seeing those reminders felt like a punch to the stomach every time they popped up.

"So what brings you to Mountain Shadow?" asked Amber over the whir of the espresso machine.

"Oh, my aunt died."

She looked up, and something like a spasm passed across her face. "Oh my god. I'm so sorry. You have, like, the *worst* luck."

I shook my head and tried to smile. "It's all right. She was my great-aunt. She was ninety-eight, so she lived a pretty good life. I'm just here to help my gran make the funeral arrangements and get her estate settled."

"That's nice of you."

In truth, I wasn't sure if I was doing Gran a favor or if it was the other way around. I couldn't stand to stay in Chicago with nothing to do but sit around trolling dating apps for anyone who looked like Todd. I needed somewhere else to focus my energy. I needed a to-do list.

"Who's your grandma?" Amber asked.

"Virginia McCrithers. She goes by Ginger, mostly. Why? Do you know her?" I knew Mountain Shadow was a small town, but I wasn't sure if it was *that* small.

Amber snorted. "Everybody knows Ginger." She waggled her eyebrows and handed over my mocha. "You're doing God's work."

An unexpected laugh burst out of me, making me forget my misery — if only for a second. I grinned and stuffed a couple of bucks into the tip jar. "Thanks for the drink. I'll see you around."

"I'm sure you will . . ." She nodded at the mocha. "I know a junkie when I see one."

I shook my head and ducked out of the coffee shop with a wave. The rain had subsided to a cold sprinkle, and I took a left at the intersection and drove up the familiar narrow street lined with candy-colored craftsman bungalows that seemed to be sliding right down the mountain.

Gran's house was situated at the end of a dead-end street, painted the same shade of robin's-egg blue that I remembered from my childhood. It was a one-story house with a big covered porch and dainty gingerbread trim painted white. An orange Ford Pinto with a little American flag on the antenna was parked in the narrow driveway.

The yard looked like some sort of a theme park/all-you-can-eat buffet for birds. Stone bird baths, hanging feeders, and whirly rainbow yard ornaments crowded the footpath leading up to the front door. The rain had nearly abated by then, and a few hummingbirds were flitting around the feeders. The sight made my chest ache with nostalgic comfort.

Grabbing my purse and my giant magenta Filofax, I headed up the front walkway. The bulky planner might have been old-fashioned, but it was how I organized my life. True, a co-worker had once called my color-coded highlighting system "borderline psychotic," but seeing things written out and organized gave me a sense of calm.

As I picked my way along the garden path, I braced myself for whatever sort of mood Gran might be in. Something had happened between her and Aunt Lucille around the time my grandpa had been killed, though no one in my family would tell me — or even seemed to know — exactly what that was. I figured Gran might be having a hard time coping with her sister's death, since she and Lucille had been on the outs.

Halfway to the door, I realized I had no client meetings to prepare for and no wedding to plan — and therefore no need for my bulky Filofax. But before I could double back to leave it in the car, the front door of the house burst open, sending the hummingbirds flying.

Gran was not a tall woman — perhaps four foot eleven in shoes. But she made up for it with the loud clothes she wore. She was resplendent in a red velour tracksuit with sparkly silver stripes along each leg. Her cloud of white hair was somewhat contained by the stretchy band of her purple rhinestone visor, and she was wearing the most enormous pair of wraparound sunglasses I'd ever seen in my life.

"Is that my granddaughter?" Gran exclaimed, peering at me from over the top of her sunglasses.

"It's me!" A wide grin spread across my face, and my whole body sagged with relief.

Gran was six years younger than Aunt Lucille, but she

was still in her nineties. I'd been worried that she'd seem older and frailer than the last time I'd visited, but she looked the same as ever.

"Good to see you, honey," Gran gushed, meeting me halfway and wrapping one bony arm around my waist.

I gave her a gentle squeeze around the shoulders, reveling in her familiar perfume of cinnamon, cloves, and clean-smelling shampoo.

"We need to get a move-on," she said in a brisk tone, pulling out of the hug and fishing around in her purse. "We're going to be late."

I glanced down at Gran's dazzling white Skechers, which were what she called her "going out" shoes. I frowned. "Late for what?"

"We're supposed to meet the attorney who was managing Lucille's estate, if I can ever find a house key."

"Oh," I said, feeling awkward. I'd received a message from Aunt Lucille's attorney two days before, telling me I'd been named in her will. In his message, the attorney had said he'd mail me a physical copy of the document, but I'd left town before it had arrived, and he'd been in court the day I'd called back to discuss the details of my inheritance.

"I need to return the rental car."

"Oh, you can do that later. Let's take the Pinto. Snowball likes the Pinto."

As if on cue, a little white dog came bounding through the open front door — a west highland terrier who, I suspected, lived better than most humans.

"Hey, Snowball!" I crooned, bending down to scratch him behind the ears. Snowball opened his mouth in a happy pant, and his big pink tongue lolled out.

"He's looking good," I told Gran, taking in his glossy white coat and bright brown eyes. "What have you been feeding him?"

Snowball hadn't been looking this good on my last visit, and I'd been worried he might not be long for this world.

"LuckyChow and Vienna sausages, mainly. That's Snowball the Fourth." Gran gestured to her front lawn, where three tasteful little resin headstones shaped like dog bones were lined up in a row.

"Oh." I grimaced. "Sorry, Gran. I didn't know. RIP, Snowball the Third."

Gran nodded solemnly and scoffed to herself. "I don't know what I did with that darn house key." She shut the door and shuffled out toward her car, moving with surprising swiftness for such an old woman. "You'll have to drive. The Colorado Department of Motor Vehicles has kindly requested that I abstain."

"From *driving*?" This was news to me. Gran had always driven herself everywhere, despite her advancing age. "Abstain until when?"

"Just until I die," she said cheerfully, opening the passenger door of her car so Snowball could hop in.

"I thought you couldn't find your keys."

"Just the house key," said Gran impatiently. "The car key's in the ignition."

"Gran, you shouldn't —"

"I keep hoping someone will steal this old thing so that I don't have to fiddle with selling it," she said in exasperation. "No such luck." Snowball hopped into the back, and Gran lowered herself into the passenger seat with a little grunt of exertion. "You know, back in my day, you couldn't leave the key in an unlocked car on Main Street without worrying that someone might steal it. But young people have gotten so lazy they don't even want to do that!"

I snorted and walked around to the driver's seat, pausing with my hand on the door handle. They wouldn't have yanked Gran's license just because of her age, would they? There had to have been some incident that had led to her license being revoked. I decided to ask her about it the next day after her soaps. She was always in a good mood then.

"Any idea why the attorney wants to see us in person rather than just mailing the will?" I asked as I climbed into the seat, which was jammed up so close to the steering wheel I had a hard time maneuvering my knees.

Gran turned to me and furrowed her brows. "Caroline, I hardly ever had any idea why Lucille did *anything*. You may not know this about your great-aunt, but she was an eccentric woman." Gran turned back toward the tiny side mirror and adjusted her rhinestone-encrusted visor. "Be glad you take after me."

CHAPTER THREE

Although Aunt Lucille had spent the last years of her life in a nursing home down in Colorado Springs, the offices of Stoger, Schwartz, and Stein were in an old three-story brick building just off First and Main.

The interior of the building looked as though it had last been remodeled sometime in the late seventies. Brown shag carpeting blanketed the reception area, and the scratchy orange upholstered chairs smelled like Pine-Sol and cigarettes.

After a kindly blond receptionist buzzed us in and offered us coffee, she led the way down a long hallway cluttered with filing cabinets and stacks of paperwork. The office of R.P. Stein, attorney at law, had the same horrendous shag carpeting and appeared to be the source of the cigarette smell.

The man sitting behind the desk was thin and gaunt and looked to be in his early seventies. He wore rimless rectangular glasses and a heavy brown suit that seemed right on theme with the decor. He was mostly bald, clean-shaven, and pale, except for his ruddy jowls. He stood up when we entered the room and came around to greet us.

"Ginger," he said in a low, fond voice, clasping Gran's bony hand in both his own. "Good to see you — well, not under the circumstances. I'm so sorry for your loss."

Gran nodded, an obligatory closed-lipped smile firmly in place.

"Snowball." R.P. gave the dog a little salute. "And this must be your granddaughter, Caroline."

"Nice to meet you," I said, reaching out to take his hand.

"Please, have a seat. Can I get you two something to drink?"

"We didn't come all this way for tea, Ronald," Gran chided, lowering herself into a chair. Snowball hopped into her lap and sat facing R.P.'s desk. "The suspense is killing me. What was so important that you had to call us down here to discuss Lucille's will in person?"

R.P. — Ronald — cleared his throat, and the corner of his mouth twitched in what I was certain was a wry smile. "You don't beat around the bush, Ginger. That's one thing I've always admired about you."

"I'm not the one paying you by the hour, Ronald," Gran shot back. "And from what I heard, after three years in that nursing home, Lucille's estate was pretty anemic. So you'd best dispense with the flattery and cut right to the chase."

R.P. looked as though he'd just swallowed a fly, but he cleared his throat and recovered quickly. "Yes, well, you are correct in that your sister was fairly cash-poor when she passed. Lucille had a small amount of savings, most of which will go toward settling her estate, but she did own an investment property and some oil interests down in Oklahoma. You two are the sole heirs mentioned in her final will and testament."

"Let's hear it, then," Gran snapped, looking suddenly dour.

R.P. swapped out his sleek rectangular specs for a pair of thick tortoise-shell ones and began to read from a long sheath of paper. *"To my great-niece, Miss Caroline McCrithers, I bequeath The Mountain Shadow Grand and my life savings in the hope that she will use what remains of my estate to restore it to its former glory."*

R.P. paused in his reading and glanced up at me over the top of his glasses. I blinked back at him dumbly. Aunt Lucille had left me some sort of property?

"The Mountain Shadow Grand is a hotel," R.P. explained, opening his desk drawer and rattling around until he produced a water-stained real-estate flyer. "Though I'm afraid it has been abandoned for some time. Lucille bought the property back in eighty-nine, I believe."

I looked down at the flyer, which showed a stately red-brick building and photos of rooms that looked as though they'd been redone sometime in the sixties. The flier said the hotel had been built in eighteen seventy-nine by Ulysses and Charles Bellwether and had operated continuously until it shuttered its doors in nineteen seventy-two.

"As I said, there is very little left of your aunt's savings." R.P. went back to rummaging in his drawer and produced a set of keys on an oblong leather keyring with "Mountain Shadow Grand" embossed on its face. "These will allow you to access the hotel."

"It's less of a hotel and more of a stopover for vagrants and local hoodlums," Gran grumbled.

"It was very dear to your aunt's heart," R.P. put in gently. "She held on to it as an investment even when it would have been more prudent to sell."

"Developers have had their eye on that property for years," said Gran. "I'm sure they would love to tear it down and slap up some overpriced condominiums and a Starlucks."

"Starbucks," I muttered.

"Whatever." Gran let out a tired sigh and turned back to R.P. "Anything else?"

The attorney cleared his throat and returned to reading the will. *"To my dear sister, Virginia McCrithers, I leave my collection of mineral deeds, as well as all my remaining earthly possessions."*

"Oh, goody. She's left me her collection of tap shoes and feather boas," Gran muttered.

"You will have to pay a visit to Sunnyview Estates to see what other personal effects Lucille left behind," R.P. replied dryly. He cleared his throat and continued reading. *"It is my deepest hope that, despite our differences, you will find it in your heart to help Caroline navigate the renovations of the hotel. You know how much it would mean to me to see it restored."*

R.P. glanced up at Gran. "The mineral deeds might be worth something once the oil companies begin drilling in that area again, but for the moment, you won't get much." He turned to me. "As for The Mountain Shadow Grand, I have some bad news."

I raised my eyebrows. How could there be *more* news? I hadn't even had a chance to absorb the fact that Aunt Lucille had left me a hotel.

"I'm afraid Lucille has been neglecting the property

taxes on The Grand for quite some time. The Colorado Department of Revenue placed a lien on the property a few years back, and someone purchased the lien."

"What do you mean someone *purchased* it?" Gran asked.

"In the state of Colorado, delinquent real-estate tax liens are sold at public auction. The original property owner has three years from the date of sale to redeem that lien — meaning they must repay the back taxes with interest and fees. If the lien is not redeemed within that time period, the individual who purchased the lien may apply for the title of the property and gain ownership."

I had the sudden thought that I should be writing all this down, so I flipped open my trusty Filofax to a blank page and began scribbling.

"Unfortunately, Lucille failed to repay the taxes while she was alive, and her death has left us little time to resolve the matter. Three years from the date of sale is one month from today. And I'm afraid that once her estate is settled, there will not be enough cash left to redeem the lien."

My heart sank. "So we have a month to come up with the money or we lose the hotel?"

"Precisely."

"How much did Aunt Lucille owe?"

"About twenty thousand dollars."

"Twenty thousand dollars?"

R.P. nodded. "Property values in Colorado have been on the rise for some time, especially here in Mountain Shadow. I'm afraid that has been to the detriment of some of our oldest residents."

I wrote *"20K?"* at the top of my notes and swallowed. I

didn't have twenty thousand dollars. I'd poured nearly every cent I had into planning the wedding. I'd thought that once Todd and I were living under one roof and sharing expenses, it would be easy to recoup my savings. What a joke that had turned out to be.

"Do you happen to know who purchased the lien?" Gran asked.

R.P. cast her a sidelong look. "As a matter of fact, I do. It's a small town," he added, somewhat apologetically. "It was Jay Mathers."

Gran looked outraged. "That weaselly developer from Denver who's been snapping up every piece of real estate he can get his greasy fingers on?"

R.P. held up his hands in a gesture of surrender. "Your words, not mine."

Gran seemed to consider this for a moment. "What if we sold the mineral deeds?"

"Those deeds may be worth that sometime in the near future, but at the moment, I doubt you'd be able to get more than a few thousand for them."

Gran frowned.

"Oh, I almost forgot," said R.P., smoothing his thumb over the sheath of oversized paper, which had a smaller scrap taped to the bottom. "Lucille added an addendum before she passed. This one concerns Caroline." R.P. glanced up at me and cleared his throat. *"To my niece, I also bequeath my cat Desmond, whom I'm sure will serve her as faithfully as he served me."*

"Cat?"

I looked to Gran for clarification, but I didn't have time to puzzle over the bizarre wording of Aunt Lucille's final addendum. As if she'd been waiting for her cue, the attorney's receptionist came striding into the room toting a small purple pet crate. A menacing yowl came from inside, along with the *scritch-scritch-scratch* of claws on plastic.

Snowball was instantly on high alert, a low growl rumbling in his throat as he stood on Gran's lap.

The receptionist set the crate on R.P.'s desk facing me, and I peered through the small cage door. Two glowing yellow eyes blinked back at me. A huge black cat was hunkered down in the back of the crate. Snowball let out an aggressive-sounding bark and continued to growl, but Gran quieted him with a few soothing strokes down his back.

For a moment, the cat and I just stared at one another, and then his yowls faded into low, gravelly purrs.

"She left me her cat?" I asked, looking up at Lucille's attorney. "Is that even *legal*?"

"Yes. And it's actually quite common," said R.P. in an amused tone.

I furrowed my brows and looked down at Desmond. I'd never had a cat — or any pet, for that matter. My mom hated any kind of mess, so I'd never been allowed so much as a hamster. As an adult, I'd always lived in an apartment building and had never even considered getting an animal.

"Well, thank you for your help, R.P.," said Gran, nudging Snowball onto the floor and rising to her feet. "It's been interesting."

"Do you have a card?" I asked, feeling suddenly frantic. "In case we have any questions?"

"Certainly," said R.P., sliding a yellowed business card across the desk. "Please don't hesitate to call if there's anything I can help you with."

Two minutes later, Gran, Snowball, Desmond, and I were all crammed into the Pinto. Snowball rode on Gran's lap with his head out the window, and I'd put Desmond's cat carrier in the back.

"I guess I need to get a litter box," I mused, still reeling from the shock of learning that Aunt Lucille had left me her cat and an old hotel. "And some cat food."

"I'm sure Lucille has all those things back in her room at Sunnyview."

"You feel like going over there to look through her things?" I asked.

"Not particularly, no."

The finality in Gran's voice told me that was the end of the conversation, so I shut my mouth and pulled away from the curb. I would need to go shopping after all.

"Where is The Mountain Shadow Grand?" I asked, half out of curiosity and half simply to break the awkward tension that seemed to have settled over the car since I'd brought up going to the nursing home.

"Oh, you've seen it. It's just up the road." Gran pointed up Main Street, and I kept driving.

"I thought Lucille was out of her mind when she bought that hotel," Gran mused. "But from what I hear, she's had developers beating down her door trying to buy it these last ten years." Another long pause. "You could probably get some decent money for it."

I turned to look at Gran, taken aback. "You think I should sell it?"

"What else are you going to do?"

I frowned. "Aunt Lucille wanted me to renovate it, I guess."

"*Renovate* it?" Gran let out a hard bark of laughter. "Maybe you haven't seen it."

I continued up the road until Gran pointed me right on Phantom Canyon Boulevard. "There," she said, pointing out her window at the towering red-brick building that loomed over downtown. The hotel was four stories with one of those vertical marquees along the side and "Mountain Shadow Grand" imposed in huge letters. All the windows were boarded up, and nearly every piece of plywood was covered in spray paint.

Taking in the crumbling facade, I realized I *had* seen the hotel before. It had been like this since I was little, but I'd scarcely noticed it on all my visits to Mountain Shadow. It stood patiently on the hill overlooking downtown — its windows dark, completely deserted.

"It was a beautiful hotel in its day," said Gran, pulling me out of my reverie. "It's a shame the place has gone to wrack and ruin. Seems to me if Lucille really cared that much, she should have made sure there was money for the renovations."

"R.P. made it sound as though she *had* left money for renovations," I pointed out. "She just never expected to drain her life savings by spending her last three years in a nursing home."

Gran shook her head. "I know what her will said, Caroline, but you're my granddaughter, and I don't want to see you go broke trying to save this old place."

"Fat chance," I muttered. "I already blew my savings on a fake wedding to a guy who was using me for my money."

Gran turned and fixed me with a long, hard look. She'd barely said two words about the cancelled wedding when I'd explained what had happened, and she didn't say anything then. She just reached over and patted me on the hand. "Shall we go in and have a look around? I haven't seen the inside of this hotel in — oh — probably sixty years."

CHAPTER FOUR

Gran sighed as she climbed out of the car, and Desmond gave a plaintive howl. Snowball wagged his tail excitedly, looking from me to Gran, and I cast a guilty glance into the back of the Pinto.

Desmond's huge yellow eyes blinked back at me, and I felt a fresh pang of remorse. After losing his person, being handed off to a couple of strangers, and forced to ride in a car with a dog, Desmond was having a worse week than I was.

Feeling sorry for the cat, I walked around to grab his crate and carried him up to the front steps of the hotel.

"You plan on leaving him here to fend for himself?" Gran asked, glancing down at the crate.

"I don't want to leave him in the car. He's been through enough as it is."

Gran just shrugged, and Desmond hissed.

"Desmond, no! Bad kitty!"

Gran snorted. "That cat never did like me very much."

"When did you ever meet him?" I asked, strangely

defensive of the animal I'd just inherited. "I thought you and Lucille had hardly spoken in the last thirty years."

Gran considered this for a moment. "That sounds about right."

I let out an incredulous laugh. "Cats don't live that long."

"I don't know when I met that wretched cat of hers, Caroline, but I'm telling you, he has *never* been particularly friendly."

I rolled my eyes and set the crate down as I fished around in my purse for the keys. Gran must have been thinking of another cat. Perhaps Lucille had picked up her sister's habit of giving all her pets the same name so she wouldn't have to remember a new one.

Desmond groused as I fumbled with the keys, searching for one that would unlock the front entrance. The heavy wooden doors looked as though they were original to the building and, incredibly, were unmarred by spray paint. Snowball sniffed around the corner where dead leaves had gathered, wagging his tail as if he couldn't wait to go inside.

I finally settled on a shiny brass key that looked more modern than the door itself and managed to coax the lock open. A draft of cold air rushed out as the door swung open, raising goosebumps all over my arms.

Despite the warm weather, it was chilly inside the building. Little motes of dust swirled in the slice of daylight pouring in, while shadows loomed in the dark. The cracks between the plywood and the edges of the windows sent darts of golden light spilling over the parquet floor, which was covered in a thick layer of dust and grit.

I reached down to let Desmond out of his crate, and he shot off across the lobby — leaving shiny little paw prints in the dust. The floorboards creaked as I stepped inside, and Gran and Snowball followed.

The lobby of The Mountain Shadow Grand looked like a place where time had stood still. The decorative plaster ceiling rose high overhead, gilded with gold paint. To my left was a sort of lounge area, and beyond that was what appeared to be a ballroom. The walls were stained yellow with nicotine and age, and the scent of mildew and old tobacco clung to every surface.

I felt along the inside wall for some kind of switch, but when I flipped it, nothing happened. The first thing I needed to do was call the city and get the power turned back on. I was itching to start my to-do list, but I'd left my trusty day planner in the car.

Flipping on my phone light, I shined it around the lobby and saw that the building was not the empty shell I'd assumed. A wooden counter stood directly across from the hotel entrance, beautifully carved with the figure of a woman holding a long staff. Behind the desk were mail slots for every room, with little brass hooks for the room keys to hang.

A dramatic curved staircase dominated the lobby, and in the far right corner was a huge birdcage elevator. The pink carpet runner on the stairs was badly stained, the wallpaper faded and peeling, but I could see how The Mountain Shadow Grand had been, well, *grand*.

An enormous grandfather clock stood guard at the foot of the stairs. One of the plinths at the base had a chunk missing, making the clock stand slightly lopsided. The front panel of glass was broken, and brass weights and chains littered the floor.

Poor clock. It was as though an axe murderer had gone to town on the thing — or, more likely, a teenager with a baseball bat. Several torn sofas were scattered around the lounge area, along with shards of ceramic and the desiccated remains of potted plants.

By the look of the place, people had been squatting in the hotel on and off for years and using the couches for who knew what. Springs stuck out of all the furniture, along with chunks of yellow stuffing. Still, I could just imagine the cozy seating area flanked by potted palms and all the stylish people who would have paraded in and out of the lobby.

Just then, Desmond streaked out from behind the front desk and led the way up the staircase with an excited *yee-ow*. Snowball, who'd been sniffing around on one of the disemboweled loveseats, hopped down and skittered after him.

I heard an angry *reee-arrr* from the floor above, followed by an excited bark. Snowball came bounding back down the steps with a whine, his tail tucked between his legs.

"Oh, Snow. Is that old cat being mean to you?" asked Gran, gripping the polished banister for support and starting up the stairs.

Snowball barked and sat back on his haunches, refusing to go any farther. Gran shot him an exasperated look, and I glanced up to find Desmond glaring imperiously down at him from the second-floor landing.

"Would you get him and bring him up?" Gran asked.

"I don't like the thought of him roaming around here by himself. He could get into something he shouldn't."

I bent down to grab Snowball, but he backed away from me with a low growl. He couldn't have weighed more than twenty pounds soaking wet, but something in that growl gave me pause.

"Snowball! Use your manners! What on earth is the matter with you?"

I made a grab for Snowball, but he nipped at my hand, backing away with his hackles raised.

"Just leave him," Gran grumbled, continuing her arduous climb. "*Oof!* If I live too much longer, I'm gonna need to have this knee redone."

"When we get the power back on, you can just use the elevator."

"No, thank you. That thing's an antique, and as an antique myself, I can tell you we sometimes don't work so good."

I swallowed a chuckle and followed Gran at a snaillike pace until we reached the top of the stairs. Shining the beam of my phone light down the long, narrow hallway, I saw that the second floor had the original wainscoting, though the walls had been repapered. The floorboards creaked underfoot as I examined the collection of black-and-white photographs decorating the walls. The glass was so filthy that it was impossible to make out any details, but I still felt the eyes of all the people in the portraits following us down the corridor.

"It says here there are twenty-seven rooms," I said, reading from the crumpled flier Lucille's attorney had given me. "The rooms on the second and third floors were updated sometime in the sixties, but the fourth floor has been closed since nineteen forty-nine and maintains most of the original features of the building."

"*Original features.*" Gran snorted. "That means it still has the old knob-and-tube wiring."

I sighed. That alone would probably cost a hundred grand to have updated. I didn't have that kind of money.

"I'm guessing nothing else about this place is up to co —" I broke off as the floor gave way beneath me. My stomach lurched as my foot sank through the rotten boards, and I stumbled and nearly fell. The leg of my jeans caught on the splintered wood, and I hissed as my ankle barked with pain.

"Are you all right?" Gran sounded alarmed.

"Fine," I said, gingerly extracting my leg from the rotten floor and staring down into the hole. "But I don't think you should be walking around up here until we know where the floor's unstable."

Looking up at the ceiling, I could see faint water stains around the light fixture. "There must have been a leak at some point," I murmured. "The floor just rotted away."

Gran didn't reply. She was already heading down the hallway in the opposite direction, poking her head in every open door. I hurried to catch up, worried for her safety. But just as I came to the door across from the stairs, I got a cold, icky feeling, like icy water being poured down my back.

I stiffened, and out of the corner of my eye, I saw something small and dark streak past me. I squealed and whipped around, and my heart flew into overdrive as I came face to face with —

I sighed. It was just an old spotted mirror. Then the

"intruder" let out a high-pitched yowl, and a pair of yellow eyes flashed in the dark.

Des.

The name echoed in my head as though someone had spoken it out loud, but Gran was already halfway down the hallway, and there was no one else around.

Deciding I must have imagined it, I put a hand over my chest to try to calm my racing heart. Snowball came scampering up the stairs to see what all the fuss was about, tearing onto the landing with a ferocious growl.

Desmond leapt deftly onto the baluster, silently taunting the dog.

"Be nice, you two," I told the animals, looking from one to the other.

Snowball's mouth fell open in an excited pant, and Desmond gave me a look that said, quite plainly, *You can't be serious.*

I shivered. There was such an intense spark of intelligence behind those yellow eyes that I could have sworn the cat understood.

"You be nice to Snowball, or I'll turn you into a hat," Gran called sternly.

Desmond made a snarky little chattering sound and pranced down the hall along the railing. Snowball followed, barking his head off, but I clicked my tongue to call him off. I knew I couldn't leave Desmond at the hotel, but it sure was tempting. He seemed right at home, and I was sure he'd make a dent in the hotel's mouse population.

Gran slipped into the room at the very end of the hall, and I followed her inside. The walls were covered in a faded floral wallpaper, and it still had what appeared to be the original crystal pendant light. A dark wood vanity with a cracked mirror stood opposite a sagging four-poster bed. The mattress was filthy and ripped to shreds. I didn't like to think what sort of critters had made The Mountain Shadow Grand their home.

Gran's head swiveled around the room, taking in the dilapidated wallpaper and battered furniture. "I always said Lucille had champagne taste and beer money."

I opened my mouth to form a reply, but just then I heard a crack of plaster, and the pendant light above our heads came crashing to the floor. Shards of glass and crystal pendeloques flew everywhere, and I looked up to see Gran standing not two feet from where it had landed.

She blinked in surprise. "I'll wear my hard hat next time. You've got your work cut out for you if you decide to keep it."

"Yeah, but how?" I sighed, tilting my head back to see if there were any more precarious hanging fixtures and getting distracted by the ornate design of the rusted tin ceiling tiles. "If what R.P. says is true, in a month the hotel will go to Jay Mathers unless I can come up with twenty thousand dollars."

Gran pursed her lips. "If it's a matter of money, I'll pay what Lucille owed in taxes."

I shook my head. "I can't ask you to do that."

"You didn't, Caroline. I'm offering. If you truly want to keep this old pile of bricks and find a way to renovate it, I'll pay off the tax lien. I just need some time to liquidate a few assets."

"But . . . why would you do that?" I asked. "I thought you said Lucille was out of her mind to buy this place."

"She was. But even a broken clock is right twice a day.

Turns out it wasn't a bad investment." She fixed me with an indulgent look. "Lucille was a lot of things, but she was also my sister. If it was her dying wish that you restore this hotel and you're willing to take up that cause, I'll help you in any way I can. Plus, I'd rather eat nails than let that rat Jay Mathers get this place for a song."

I snorted. That sounded a lot more like the Gran I knew. She was always railing about the greedy developers from Denver and elsewhere who'd been buying up Mountain Shadow real estate. I knew that if I did let the hotel go, Mathers or someone like him would eventually buy it just so that they could tear it down. I couldn't let that happen. This place must have meant a great deal to Aunt Lucille for her to hold on to it all this time.

"I'll pay you back," I promised, "with interest."

"You'll do no such thing," Gran replied. "You're *young*, Caroline. This business with that Todd fellow may have thrown you for a loop, but someday you're going to meet a nice man you want to marry. Then the two of you may want to buy a house . . . gift me with a great-grandchild or two . . ."

I rolled my eyes.

"Those things cost money, and I've got *more* than enough to coast through my golden years in style." She paused, her eyes glimmering with mischief. "I'll just deduct it from your inheritance."

CHAPTER FIVE

The next morning, I was awoken by the deep, sultry voice of Billy Blanks and the truly alarming sound of Gran's advanced Tae Bo workout.

Count it! One . . . two . . . three. Work it. Seven . . . eight . . . nine . . . ten.

I opened my eyes and came face to face with the army of creepy ceramic bunnies lined up on the windowsill. Beside the window stood an old rocking chair with a Raggedy Ann doll and a teddy bear that was missing one eye.

With different lighting, Gran's decor wouldn't have been out of place in a horror movie. But with the early-morning sunshine coming in through the gauzy white curtains, it felt pleasantly homey.

I wiggled my legs, which were trapped in a straight-jacket of a patchwork quilt, and found something warm and round wedged behind my knees. Desmond was curled up in a ball beside me, his paws tucked neatly against his chest.

Ree-ow.

"What are *you* doing up here?" I asked, glaring down at him. I'd made him a bed in the corner of the room, but that clearly hadn't been good enough.

Out in the living room, I heard Gran moving around and lowered my voice to a whisper. "You're not supposed to be on the furniture. If Gran catches you . . ."

The cat just blinked at me as if this sounded like a me-and-Gran problem rather than a Desmond problem. Seeing that he wasn't going to move on his own, I shoved him over a few inches and tried to go back to sleep, but the sound of eighties workout music blared through the thin walls.

Moaning and groaning, I reached for my phone and immediately set it back down when I saw the notifications crowding my screen.

3:00 p.m. Dress fitting
6:00 p.m. Dinner with Todd
8:00 p.m. Finalize wedding guest list

No fiancé. No wedding — and I had a crumbling hundred-and-forty-year-old hotel to renovate on zero budget and a haughty black cat to keep me company.

My life was going great.

Peeling myself out of bed, I shuffled miserably out into the living room. Gran was already dressed for the day in another astonishing jewel-toned tracksuit. This one was made of teal windbreaker fabric that swished as she marched in place. She was moving along with a grainy VHS tape featuring a young Billy Blanks in an electric-blue bodysuit that showed off his glistening bare pecs.

"Morning, Gran," I yawned.

"Oh, you're up!" she replied. "I hope the TV didn't wake you."

"It did," I said cheerily. "But I needed to get up anyway. Lots to do."

There. That sounded productive and healthy, didn't it?

Gran nodded and flicked off the TV, bustling into the kitchen to join me. "What do you want for breakfast?"

"Coffee."

"That's not breakfast."

I shrugged. "It's what I usually have."

Gran gave me a disapproving look. "No wonder you're so high-strung."

I bristled at her blunt assessment, but Gran had already bent down and was rummaging in the cabinet. She emerged with an ancient-looking ten-speed blender and heaved it onto the counter. "How about a protein shake?"

"Is it plant-based?"

"Plant-*what*?" Gran asked, bustling over to the fridge.

"Never mind."

I watched in fascination as Gran poured whole milk into the blender, along with what looked like half a cup of Hershey's syrup.

"Gran, that's not a protein shake. That's just chocolate milk."

"It's got protein, hasn't it?"

"Yeah, but —" The deafening grind of the blender cut off my protests, and I realized I probably wasn't going to find any coffee at Gran's. I decided I'd make a quick pit stop at Déjà Brew on the way to Sunnyview Estates.

By the time I'd dressed, Gran had already downed her "protein shake" and swapped her sequined sweatband for another rhinestone visor. I left Desmond snoozing on the bed, and Gran, Snowball, and I piled into the Pinto and drove down the pass to Colorado Springs.

When we pulled up in front of Sunnyview Estates, I had to check my navigation app to be sure we had the right address. Rather than some sprawling Victorian building with a wraparound porch filled with seniors in rocking chairs, we were looking up at a squat tan building just off of I-25.

There was nothing sunny or estate-like about it. A few sad trees were slowly dying in the medians between parking rows, and an empty bird feeder swung in the breeze. A wrought-iron fence wound around the narrow dirt yard in front of the building, as though it were some minimum-security prison rather than a home for the elderly.

The moment we walked through the door, the stench of cafeteria food and industrial cleaner hit me like a ton of bricks. A woman in pink scrubs smiled warmly at Gran before turning her attention to me. "Can I help you?"

"We're not stayin'," Gran replied loudly, "so don't get any funny ideas."

The woman, to her credit, didn't seem taken aback by Gran's blunt reply. She kept her bright smile firmly in place.

"We're here to claim Lucille Blackthorne's belongings," I told her.

"Are you next of kin?"

"She was my sister," said Gran.

"Of course. I'm so sorry for your loss. I'll take you to our administrator, and she can get you squared away."

Gran gave a curt nod, though she didn't soften her demeanor. She just glanced down the hallway to our right, which was crowded with men and women parked along the wall in wheelchairs, and then to a large open room, where a few residents were passed out in front of a television. I couldn't imagine how she was feeling, thinking of her sister in a place like this.

"We're going to miss Lucille around here," the nurse told me over her shoulder as she led us down the opposite hall. "And that cat of hers." She dropped her voice. "I've been here for ten years, and between you and me, we had a bit of a pest problem before Lucille and Desmond moved in."

She turned away, and I wrinkled my nose. "You don't say?"

"Yep. Then, overnight, those mice started dropping like flies." The nurse let out a girlish laugh, and my stomach did a nasty flop.

"Between you and me," said Gran, "it looks like things are *still* dropping like flies, only it's not the mice."

The nurse turned, mouth hanging open, but just then another woman materialized from some back office. She introduced herself with a smile that didn't quite meet her eyes and then asked Gran to sign some paperwork so they could release Lucille's belongings.

Once everything was in order, the woman led us down another hallway, past rooms with open doors, where people were sleeping or being helped into wheelchairs. What bothered me more than the underlying scent of urine and human bodies was the total lack of privacy in the place.

Gran's face seemed to harden with every step. I kept my gaze fixed straight ahead, sad for these people who'd been forced to leave their homes and come here to live out the last of their days.

"Were you and your sister close?" asked the administrator.

"Do you think I would have let her stay here if we were?" Gran snapped.

The administrator swallowed but didn't reply.

I was ashamed to admit I hadn't visited my Aunt Lucille since she'd moved to Sunnyview. Most of my memories of her had been visiting the rambling Queen Anne on Main Street that had been converted to townhomes. Aunt Lucille's place had been a narrow two-story apartment with a tiny door at the top of the stairs that led to a hidden playroom.

As a young woman, Lucille had gotten her start as a burlesque dancer. She'd sung and danced for years before getting her "big break" as an actress. She'd starred in a couple films in the late forties and fifties and later acted in several Broadway shows.

Even in her seventies and eighties, Lucille had been larger than life. Every time I'd come to her house, she'd let me dress up in all her old costumes and entertained me with stories of her time in Hollywood.

"This was Lucille's room," said the administrator, gesturing toward the open door at the very end of the hall.

Swallowing down my nerves, I walked into the room and immediately felt my insides constrict. The only furniture in the room was a twin bed, a fake-wood wardrobe, and a battered chest of drawers. Shabby pink curtains hung over the windows, and there was a hospital call button on the wall.

A *Sunset Boulevard* poster was taped over the bed. The

rest of the available wall space was taken up by framed playbills from all the productions Lucille had ever starred in, along with several black-and-white photos of Lucille in her burlesque getup posing with people I didn't know.

The image of my lively and charming great-aunt beaming down at me in this sad little room was enough to bring tears to my eyes. Here was a woman who'd really lived, and yet she'd died *here*.

"I'll leave you to it," said the administrator, ducking down the hall.

An uncomfortable silence stretched out between me and Gran as we took in the tiny little room. I wasn't sure what the protocol was for claiming a deceased loved one's belongings. Was it appropriate to go through everything there, or were we supposed to simply box everything up and take it home to be sorted later?

Feeling awkward, I cracked the door of the wardrobe across from the bed and rifled through Lucille's clothes. They were your typical old-lady outfits — pastel nightgowns, a few house coats, and some sweaters and pants. Lucille had been nearly a head taller than her sister, so I didn't think Gran would have any use for this stuff.

Closing the wardrobe, I took a moment to absorb the sheer volume of playbills on the walls — everything from *1776* to *West Side Story*. "She really lived a full life, huh?"

"That she did," said Gran. She hadn't moved from her place by the door. She just stood there, holding her purse tight to her side, examining the black-and-white photos.

I drifted over to the huge steamer trunk under the window, which I hadn't noticed at first. A fuzzy cat bed lay on top. I'd take that back for Desmond.

Removing the bed, I cracked the lid of the trunk, and a

familiar smell washed over me. It was a mix of strong floral perfume, tobacco, and cosmetics that I automatically associated with Aunt Lucille. A clump of pale pink feathers caught my eye, and I threw the top the rest of the way open.

The trunk was filled with the types of outfits I remembered trying on as a kid — sequined dresses, hot-pink pumps, feather boas, and neon leotards. Grinning, I turned to Gran to ask if I could have one of Lucille's old costumes, but Gran was still standing by the door, stuffing a tissue into her purse.

"Let's go, Caroline."

"Go?" I glanced around in confusion. "But we just got here. Don't you want to go through her things and pick out a few —"

"No," said Gran. "I'm very tired. We can come back another day."

I hesitated and then got to my feet, shutting the lid of the steamer trunk. Gran turned to leave without another word.

I followed her out, grabbing the bed for Desmond on my way, along with a small scratching post from the wall by the bathroom.

On our way out of the building, I muttered a hurried explanation to the first nurse we'd met, hoping they would hold Lucille's things for a few more days until I could coax Gran into returning.

GRAN DIDN'T WANT to go home after we'd visited Sunnyview Estates, and it was still too early for lunch. It was the point in the day when I would usually be downing my fourth cup of coffee, but Gran was more of a tea person, so I turned onto Phantom Canyon Boulevard and pulled up in front of World's Cup Tearoom and Emporium.

The old building across from The Grand had been built around the same time period and had stately arched windows and an intricate red-brick cornice. The door of the tearoom was painted black, and the leaves of potted plants snaked along the bottom of all the windows. On the other end of the building was a run-down bar with loud music drifting from the entrance.

As soon as we walked into the tearoom, I was hit by the earthy aroma of tea, along with the more pungent, smoky smell of incense. Anemic morning sunlight filtered through the dusty windows into the main area, which was crowded with an assortment of rickety round tables. A gold statue of Ganesha sat on a pedestal by the window as an electric fountain bubbled in the corner.

Upon first glance, the cluttered, exotic tearoom didn't seem like Gran's sort of place, and I wondered if I'd made a mistake in bringing her there. But then Gran plopped down in one of the spindly wooden chairs, and a slight man with huge round glasses and salt-and-pepper hair appeared to take our order.

"Good afternoon, ladies. How are we doing today?"

"We're doing fine, Dana. Thank you for asking," said Gran, offering him a tired smile. "This is my granddaughter, Caroline. Caroline, this is Dana Marzetti."

Mr. Marzetti must have been the owner of the tearoom, I thought. He was dressed in carefully pressed brown slacks, a button-up shirt, and a fussy little orange bowtie.

Everything about him was small and fragile, and he had a precise, careful air about him.

"Pleasure to meet you," said Dana with a sincere bow of his head. "What can I get you ladies to drink?"

Gran fished her reading glasses out of her purse and picked up a tea list printed on thick linen paper. "What do you recommend?"

"It depends what you're in the mood for. I'm partial to the sturdy Fujian oolong, myself. This one has a bit of a nutty aroma." Dana pointed at an item on the list. "But right now, I have a lovely Fukamushi sencha tea from the Shizuoka prefecture in Japan — very delicate, very nice, with just the *hint* of rose petals. I also just returned from India with a wonderful Nilgiri. Very smooth, slightly fruity — typical of teas grown in that region. Or, if that doesn't appeal, I have a bold Maghrebi mint —"

"I'll try the oolong today," said Gran, handing the tea list back with a tight smile.

"Same," I said. I didn't know anything about tea, and I felt as though I knew even less after listening to Dana prattle on. He gave a quick bow and bustled back behind the counter.

Once he was out of earshot, I finally asked the question that had been rubbing at the back of my mind ever since we'd left the nursing home.

"Gran?"

"Hmm?"

"What happened with you and Aunt Lucille?"

Gran looked startled and then irritated and picked up the tea list again. "I'm very tired, Caroline. I don't think now is the best time to discuss it."

"Well, we have to discuss it *sometime*."

"No, we don't. I am ninety-two years old, Caroline. I don't have a job or any living children, and your grandfather is dead. The only thing I *have* to do is pay my taxes and die."

I let out a huff. Gran could be so stubborn. And when she really dug her heels in on something, there was no point in trying to fight her. I decided to try another tack.

"Gran, Aunt Lucille's dead. Don't you think it's time to let all that go?"

At those words, Gran's upper lip puckered in a stern expression, and she fixed me with a hawklike stare that raised the hairs along the back of my neck. "What happened between me and my sister is between Lucille and me. I don't know why you're so determined to stir it all up!"

"Because it's clearly still bothering you."

"That's my business!"

I sighed. "Gran, she was your *sister*."

"So that means I'm not allowed to be angry with her?"

"No, but —" I broke off. I knew trying to get her to talk about Aunt Lucille was a losing proposition. Gran had been a farm girl during the Great Depression and had lived through World War II. She could slaughter a chicken without batting an eye and reuse the same piece of aluminum foil until it fell apart, but talking about her feelings wasn't going to happen.

Luckily, Dana reappeared at that moment carrying a tray laden with a squat clay teapot and two matching handle-less cups.

Gran thanked him and poured us both some tea, settling back in her chair with a sigh.

"Now," she said, "since you're so keen on sticking your

nose into *my* business, why don't you tell me what happened with that young man you were so sweet on?"

I groaned. I should have known that Gran would find a way to change the subject.

"I already told you," I said. "Todd lied. He wasn't interested in me. He was only dating me so he could bilk me out of the money for the wedding."

"And you *fell* for that?" Gran scoffed. "I would have thought my granddaughter had more sense than to be taken in by a phony like that!"

At those words, my stomach burned with an acrid shame that was becoming far too familiar. When Todd had skipped town with all my money, I'd had to tell the whole story at least a couple dozen times — to the police, my bank, the credit-card company, the people who managed my apartment building, friends, wedding guests, co-workers, the lady who worked the front desk at my gym . . .

I'd rehashed the story so many times it had started not to feel real — until then.

"I screwed up, okay?" I muttered sheepishly. "I guess my instincts aren't as good as I thought they were."

"Instincts haven't got anything to do with it," said Gran. "You saw what you wanted to see — plain and simple."

"I guess."

Gran nodded. "It's the same with Lucille, you know."

I frowned. "I'm not sure I follow."

"To you, she was this exciting and dramatic person who lived as though all the world was a stage. But as a sister, she could be flighty, capricious, and impulsive. Once I left home, I was always cleaning up her messes." Gran took a sip of her tea and set down her cup in exasperation.

"I won't go into the hairy details of my problem with your aunt. I'll just say this: At some point, Lucille did what Lucille *always* did, and I bailed her out for the last time."

I chewed on the inside of my cheek. Gran's cryptic explanation left me with more questions than answers, but I knew she wouldn't tell me any more if I asked, so I just waited for her to continue.

"Every action has consequences, Caroline," said Gran. "Some I'm sure Lucille couldn't have foreseen."

CHAPTER SIX

Although I'd intended to wake up early on Friday to make some phone calls about the hotel, sunlight was streaming in through the curtains by the time I peeled my eyelids open. The house smelled like ginger and molasses, and Desmond was once again nestled in the crook of my legs.

"You're not supposed to be up here," I murmured.

Desmond stared up at me with a blasé expression, and I reached down to scratch him behind the ears.

"This is the last time," I whispered. "Tonight you have to sleep in your bed." I cast a pointed glance at the fuzzy cat bed I'd brought back from the nursing home, but Desmond merely gave a bored yawn and stretched out his legs in front of him.

I rolled out of bed and pulled on some clothes, wandering out into the living room in search of Gran. Billy Blanks wasn't on the TV that morning, and the blender pitcher wasn't soaking in the sink. Snowball was gone, and Gran's Skechers weren't sitting by the front door, so I figured she'd gone out for a walk.

Thinking I needed caffeine to start my day off on the right foot, I slipped into my flats and pulled on my jean jacket. I'd just swing by Déjà Brew for a pick-me-up latte and a pastry for Gran, and then I'd get to work calling contractors and the funeral home to start making arrangements for Aunt Lucille.

But just as I was about to head out, Desmond came prancing down the hallway after me and stood by the door, as if waiting to be let out.

"Your litterbox is in there," I told him, pointing at the open door to the laundry room.

Ree-ow.

"You're not an outside cat. You stay in here while I'm gone."

Ree-ow. Des reached up and pawed at my leg, his little claws snagging on my cherry-red skinny jeans.

"Ow! No. You can't come with me."

Those huge golden eyes blinked up at me intently, and I let out an exasperated sigh. "If I had a kitty harness, I'd take you with me, but I don't."

Maybe I was imagining things, but I could have sworn that Desmond scowled at the mention of a kitty harness.

"We'll talk about it later," I assured him.

Why was I negotiating with a cat? I wondered. Clearly I'd lost my mind.

Ignoring Desmond's whines of protest, I slipped out the front door without bothering to lock it behind me. Gran had left me asleep in an unlocked house, so I figured home security wasn't her top priority.

By then the sun had risen fully, and I could feel the heat

through my jacket. It warmed my face and woke me up as I walked down the hill. I hung a right on Main Street and kept walking toward Déjà Brew, but just then a black SUV came tearing down the street.

Brakes squealed as the SUV veered right, and for a moment I thought it might run me over. But just as the front right tire banked up over the curb, the vehicle came to a sudden halt, and a man staggered into the street.

I opened my mouth, but no words came out. The man looked to be in his midfifties — clean-shaven, slightly chubby, and well-dressed with olive skin and neatly shorn dark hair. At first, I thought the man might be drunk, but his movements were too stiff and jerky.

Wheezing, the man fell to his knees in the middle of the road, back arching as if in pain. He tilted his head back, tendons bulging, and for a moment I thought he was choking.

I fumbled in my pockets to call nine-one-one, but I didn't have my phone.

"Help!" I cried, looking up and down the street. "Somebody call an ambulance!"

A couple standing outside the café murmured in alarm, and I stumbled off the curb and approached the man slowly. His face was turning an alarming shade of purple, and he looked as though he were suffering from lockjaw.

I took another step forward, but he shuffled away from me on his knees, holding out a hand to keep me back.

A horrible choking noise escaped his throat, and then he collapsed in the street. He arched his back, still making that awful noise. Then he went utterly still.

For several seconds, I couldn't hear anything except the sound of my own breathing. The world seemed to slow down, and I was vaguely aware of a man in a Hawaiian shirt rushing past me to administer CPR. He yelled something at the woman who was with him, who picked up her phone to dial nine-one-one.

Somebody touched my arm and asked if I knew the man. I just shook my head.

An odd rushing sound filled my ears as I stared at the palm fronds stretching across the man's back as he administered CPR.

Not long after, the wail of sirens cut through my haze. An ambulance, fire truck, and two police cruisers rolled up Main Street. Medics quickly surrounded the man, and the scene became a blur of commotion.

By then, a small crowd had gathered on the street — mostly tourists out for breakfast. I spotted Amber, the barista from Déjà Brew, watching from the open door of the café.

"*Caroline?*"

I turned automatically toward the sound of my name and was relieved to see Gran standing on the sidewalk. She was dressed in a purple velvet tracksuit, with Snowball trailing close behind.

"Gran," I choked.

"What are you doing out here? What's all the commotion?"

"That man, he just —" I pointed toward the street, where a group of medics were bent over the stranger. I couldn't see the man's face, but his lower body was ominously still.

"What happened?"

"I don't know. I just —"

"Excuse me, ma'am," came a smooth, authoritative voice to my left.

I looked over to see a police officer pushing his way through the mass of bodies crowded together on the sidewalk. I shuffled over to clear a path but found myself caught by a pair of striking light-blue eyes. "Ma'am?"

Was he talking to *me*?

The officer in question couldn't have been more than a few years older than me — definitely in his early thirties. He had golden-blond hair cut military short, a strong jaw, and a cleft chin. His little gold name badge read "W. Hamby," though it should have said "V. Handsome" for "very handsome."

"Officer Hamby, Mountain Shadow P.D. Do mind if I ask you a few questions?"

I blinked stupidly up at the cute policeman, swimming in those dazzling blue eyes. "Me?"

The officer nodded. "The man who administered CPR said you witnessed Mr. Mathers's collapse?"

I nodded. Mathers, Mathers . . . Why did that name sound so familiar?

"Mathers?" Gran quipped. "As in *Jay* Mathers?" She leaned to the side to try to see around the medics, who had gone abruptly still.

"Yes, ma'am." Officer Hamby turned toward Gran, brow furrowed in suspicion.

Suddenly I remembered how I knew that name. Jay Mathers was the sleazy developer who'd bought the tax lien on The Mountain Shadow Grand.

"Is he . . . he isn't *dead*?" Gran asked.

"I'm afraid so, ma'am."

"He's dead?" I whispered, heart thudding against my ribs. "But he was just . . ." I swallowed.

I'd just watched a man *die*? It didn't make sense. He'd been totally alive just a few minutes before . . .

"I-I was just walking to grab a coffee when he drove up," I stammered. "I thought he was going to hit me, he was driving so fast. But then he stopped and got out and —" I broke off. "He looked like he was choking or . . . or having some sort of fit."

Officer Hamby nodded and scribbled something on a handheld notepad. His expression was serious but not unkind.

"He s-stumbled into the road," I explained. "I thought maybe I could help him, but he held up a hand like he wanted me to stay back. Then he just sort of . . . collapsed. I would have called nine-one-one, but I didn't have my phone."

Officer Hamby nodded and stared down at his notes, rubbing his forehead with the hand that held the pen. "Was there anyone else in the car with him?"

"No. I mean, not that I saw. I was pretty distracted, though."

The officer looked up, a slight crease working its way across his smooth tan forehead. "Did you happen to know Mr. Mathers?"

I shook my head. "I'm not from around here. I'm just visiting for my aunt's funeral." I jerked my thumb toward Gran. "My grandmother might have known him."

Gran shook her head. "We've met, but I don't know him. Well, I know of his *reputation*."

Officer Hamby quirked an eyebrow. "Which is?"

"Oh, you know. He's one of those developer sharks

from Denver," said Gran. Her voice was light and casual — a little *too* casual, considering our all-too-personal connection with the late Mr. Mathers.

"Could I get your name?" asked Hamby. "I need it for my report."

"Caroline McCrithers. This is my gran, Virginia."

Something like recognition lit Hamby's eyes as he jotted down Gran's name. He glanced back at me. "And you're sure you didn't see anyone else with Mr. Mathers?"

"I'm sure." But something about his tone gave me pause. I'd never seen anyone die before, but somehow I got the feeling that they didn't ask random passersby so many questions when someone had a heart attack or a stroke. It was almost as if he thought there was something amiss about the way Mr. Mathers had died.

I glanced back at the black SUV, which still had its engine running. The windows weren't tinted, and the sun was shining. Surely I would have seen if there'd been someone in the vehicle with him.

"Is she free to go, *detective*, or are you going to ask her to dinner first?" Gran asked in a tone of good-natured exasperation.

Horror lanced through me at the question, and I felt my cheeks heat up. Officer Hamby cleared his throat, and I quickly looked down at my shoes. I swear, if the woman hadn't been in her ninth decade of life, I would've slapped her.

"I think that's all for now," he said, recovering in record time. "And I'm not a detective, ma'am. But if you wouldn't mind writing down your contact information, I'd sure appreciate it." Officer Handsome handed me his notepad and pen, and I took them without meeting his gaze. "Just in case I think of anything else."

"'Atta boy," said Gran with a wink.

I thought I might combust with embarrassment at that point, so I was glad to have something to do. As I printed my name, phone number, and email address on a clean sheet of paper, I chanced a quick glance up at Officer Hamby's face and was relieved to see that the tops of his cheeks were also a little pink.

I handed him back his notebook and pen, and he cleared his throat before excusing himself. I grimaced as I watched him cut through the crowd of onlookers to rejoin the other officers.

"Let's get outta here," said Gran, leading Snowball out of the crowd. "When you get to be my age, you don't want to hang around ambulances too long. They might throw you in by mistake."

CHAPTER SEVEN

Officer Hamby didn't call the next day or the day after — not that I'd expected him to. I'd told him everything I'd seen, which wasn't much, and it wasn't as though I expected him to call me for any *other* reason.

Still, it was hard to concentrate on planning Aunt Lucille's memorial service when I'd watched a man die in the middle of Main Street. I'd replayed the scene over and over all weekend as I'd packed up Lucille's belongings.

Gran had wanted no part in deciding what to keep, nor was she much help in planning the funeral. She'd suggested leaving Aunt Lucille's body on a mountaintop to be eaten by crows, but I was pretty sure sky burials weren't legal in the state of Colorado, so I was on my own.

By Monday morning, I'd had my fill of shopping for headstones and editing Lucille's obituary. Fortunately, I had an appointment with a general contractor to discuss the renovation of The Mountain Shadow Grand. I still didn't know how I was going to come up with the money, but I figured I'd need to secure some bids to have any idea how much I'd need.

After a hasty breakfast, I poured myself a huge thermos of coffee and drove Gran's Pinto to the hotel. This time, I let Desmond come with me. We'd returned home the day before to find he'd nibbled the leaves off all of Gran's houseplants and "rearranged" her collection of ceramic bunnies, so he could not be trusted.

The contractor was already waiting when we pulled up in front of the hotel. A huge white truck was parked along the curb, and I could see a broad-shouldered man staring up at the structure with what could only be dollar signs in his eyes.

Feeling flustered, I threw the car into park, killed the engine, and scrambled out with my trusty day planner in hand. I'd intended to arrive at the hotel early so that I could collect myself and have my questions ready. Instead, I was five minutes late.

Desmond hopped out of the car and pranced up the sidewalk ahead of me, tail held high. I'd never met a cat who could be walked off-leash like a dog, but Des showed no signs of fleeing.

"Good morning," I said, scurrying up to meet the contractor.

"Morning!"

The man was a lot taller than me and looked to be in his midforties. He wore clean work pants with his shirt tucked in, and when I took his hand to shake it, his huge rough paw swallowed my own.

"Thank you for agreeing to meet me," I said.

"No problem. I assume you're the owner?"

"Uh . . . yeah. I'm Caroline McCrithers. My great-aunt just passed away and left me the hotel."

"Miles Briggs. I'm sorry for your loss. This is some pile of bricks you've got here."

I heaved a sigh. "Yeah, it is."

Miles grinned and extended an arm, inviting me to lead the way. I took a deep breath as I fished out the key, fumbling for a moment with the lock. Desmond skirted between my legs and slinked inside ahead of us, disappearing into the gloom with a yowl.

"Some cat you've got there," said Miles from behind me.

"He's . . . something, all right. Another gift from my aunt."

"Ah."

The dusty, musty smell of the place hit me harder than it had on my first visit. The lobby was cool despite the July heat, and I noticed a few cracks in the ceiling that I could have sworn hadn't been there before. Cobwebs hung from every nook and cranny, and the floor sagged toward the middle.

Miles let out a long, slow whistle, the thud of his heavy work boots echoing in the cavernous space.

"It needs a lot of work," I admitted.

"Sure does," said Miles, not sounding at all deterred. He pivoted slowly on the spot, taking in the decaying opulence of the tall ceiling, parquet floors, and huge grand staircase. "What plans do you have for the place?"

I let out a *pfft* of air. "Well, it was my aunt's dying wish that I restore the hotel to its former glory."

Miles's eyebrows crept toward his hairline. "That's gonna cost a pretty penny."

"I figured."

"Most developers would just level the place and start from the ground up — put in some high-dollar condos, maybe a mixed-use building. I think that's what Jay Mathers had planned when he scooped up the tax lien."

My stomach clenched. Did *everyone* in this town know about my aunt's financial troubles?

Then I remembered the look of terror in Mathers's eyes as he'd collapsed on the pavement, and my insides twisted for another reason. It seemed a terrible coincidence that Mathers had died just as our time to redeem the tax lien was about to run out.

Before I could get lost on that dark train of thought, Miles clapped his hands together. "Let's have a look around, shall we?"

"Sure. We'll have to take the stairs, though. I'm afraid I haven't gotten the utilities back on yet."

"Not a problem," said Miles gamely.

"I don't suppose you know a guy who can service that old elevator?" I asked, pointing toward the far corner of the lobby.

He chuckled. "There are only a handful of functioning birdcage elevators west of the Mississippi — and only one person I'd recommend you have touch it. Name's Rusty Coleman. I'll give you his number, but I wouldn't get my hopes up. Rusty's dang hard to get ahold of."

My heart sank, but I opened my Filofax and scribbled down the name.

"If I were you, I'd have that old relic removed and replaced with something more modern to save yourself the headache."

I smiled, though privately I felt it would be a travesty

to junk one of the few functioning birdcage elevators for the sake of convenience. I led the way up the grand staircase, wincing as the steps creaked and sagged under Miles's considerable weight. I hoped the whole thing wasn't about to come crashing down beneath our feet.

I showed him the area upstairs where the floor had rotted away, and he ripped up a few of the crumbling boards to examine the floor joists beneath.

Miles took his time drifting in and out of the guest rooms, snapping photos, tapping on walls, and jotting down notes on a metal clipboard. I followed him into one of the bathrooms, which was dominated by a filthy rust-stained tub. Several ceiling tiles were missing, and I heard that little cash register in my head go *cha-ching*.

There was almost nothing in the old hotel that didn't need to be fixed or replaced. The floors sagged, the plumbing was bad, and it looked as though we had termites.

The third floor was in a similar condition to the second. Miles found water damage in one of the guest bathrooms that was the likely culprit for the leak that had led to the rotten floorboards. Once he was finished taking notes and snapping pictures, we walked down the hall to the door that concealed the stairway to the fourth floor.

I turned the knob, but the door was locked, and I remembered what the realty flyer had said about the top floor being blocked off.

Reaching into my back pocket, I pulled out the key ring R.P. had given me and examined all of them for one that might fit the lock. No such luck. All the keys I'd been given were modern brass ones, but this door clearly took a very large skeleton key.

"I-I'm sorry," I stammered. "I don't think I have a key to this door."

"That's all right," said Miles, still in that easygoing manner of his. "These old locks are a breeze to pick."

He went to grab something from his truck and returned a moment later with a set of Allen wrenches. I watched in awe as he got down on one knee, inserted a wrench, and wiggled it slightly. Then he eased a second one in and turned it clockwise like a key. Two seconds later, I heard a soft *click*, and the knob twisted without a fuss.

The door creaked loudly as he pushed it open, and the scent of moth balls, mildew, and old tobacco wafted toward me. It was pitch black inside the stairwell, but Miles produced a small flashlight from his pocket and shined it up the stairs.

"Ladies first," he said, holding the door open with his free hand.

I started up the creaky wooden steps but froze when I felt a spider web on my face. I grimaced and reached up to wipe it away, feeling a certain sense of awe.

When was the last time someone had been up here? I wondered. The dark wainscoting, the peeling wallpaper, the frosted-glass bulbs in the tarnished brass sconces — none of it had been touched since the forties. The fixtures had probably been converted to electric from their original kerosene sometime in the early eighteen nineties, and the floor hadn't been rewired. It was both breathtaking and overwhelming.

As I came to the top of the stairs, I hugged my arms tightly around me to ward off the sudden chill. The hallway was narrower up there and strewn with spiderwebs. The meager beam of Miles's flashlight bounced from one wall to the other, illuminating more black-and-white portraits coated in a thick film of dust.

Miles paused to clear one of the frames with the edge of his sleeve, and I choked as an errant dust mote lodged somewhere in the back of my throat. Coughing loudly, I took a step back and jumped as the feeling of icy-cold water seeped through my shirt.

I lifted my gaze to the ceiling, searching for more water damage. There must have been a leak. But when I reached up and felt the back of my shirt, the fabric wasn't wet.

Wheeling around, I caught a flash of movement in a spotted brass-framed mirror. Two reflections stared back at me — one pale and blond with frizzy curls and the other —

I sucked in a gasp and backed away as a familiar head of dark-brown curls bobbed somewhere over my shoulder. Her big green eyes were framed by thick dark lashes, and her face was heavily made up.

As the realization hit me, I shuffled back — bumping into Miles — and nearly crashed into the opposite wall. Miles reached out to steady me with a calm little "whoa," turning to face the mirror. As he did, Lucille's reflection vanished, replaced by Miles's friendly face.

"Are you all right?"

I didn't reply. I was still staring at the place where Aunt Lucille's face had just been, breathing hard and fast. My heart was crashing against my ribcage, and my voice caught in my throat.

That hadn't been Aunt Lucille from my most recent memory. The last time I'd visited, Lucille had been frail and stooped. Her hair had been a wiry gray, though her emerald eyes still held that same vivacious twinkle.

No. This Lucille was the Lucille from her photos — her curly dark hair coiffed in victory rolls, her skin bright and unwrinkled.

"Fine," I managed after a long while, still staring into the mirror where her reflection had been.

"You look like you've seen a ghost!"

I swallowed to wet my parched throat. "I-I haven't been sleeping well the last few nights."

"Oh, yeah. I heard you were there when ol' Mathers dropped dead."

"Yeah. I think I'm just . . . tired."

Miles nodded sympathetically. "Well, look. These types of jobs are difficult to bid, because we never really know what we're going to find once we start pulling trim and cutting into walls. I need to —"

At that moment, my phone buzzed in my pocket. I pulled it out and glanced at the screen. *Unknown number.*

Thinking it might be Officer Handsome calling, I shot Miles an apologetic look. "Excuse me. I should take this." I hit the green button to accept the call and brought the phone to my ear. "Hello?"

"Caroline?" It was Gran, but she didn't sound like herself. My heart gave a little jolt.

"Yeah, Gran. It's me. Everything all right?"

"Everything's fine, Caroline," said Gran in a tone of exaggerated patience that suggested I was a ninny for asking. "I just need you to call R.P. Stein."

"Lucille's attorney? Why? What's wrong?"

There was a long pause, though I could hear voices and what sounded like a phone ringing in the background.

"Gran . . . where are you?" I asked, suddenly suspicious.

"It's no big deal, Caroline. I just need you to call R.P. Stein. I don't have his number, and no one here has a phonebook, apparently. Tell him I'm down at the police station and that I could use his help."

CHAPTER EIGHT

The Mountain Shadow Police Department was buzzing with activity when I burst into the lobby. A woman and her teenaged son were speaking to the receptionist through the glass window, and two more young ne'er-do-wells in ripped jeans and skater shoes were slumped in plastic chairs.

If there was any doubt that the small-town police department was in desperate need of funding, one look at the shabby station put it to rest. The walls were lined with fake-wood paneling, the puke-colored tile was chipped and broken in places, and the entire station reeked of old coffee and Xerox.

As the door slammed shut behind me, the woman working the front desk looked around in alarm. "I'll be with you in just a minute."

I sighed and got in line behind the mother and son, tapping my foot impatiently as the receptionist explained, in painstaking detail, how they could appeal the son's traffic violation. Finally the pair shuffled off, and I hurried up to the window.

"Can I help you?" asked the woman behind the desk.

"I'm here to get my grandmother, Virginia McCrithers."

I said it all in one breath, and an uneasy look flashed through the receptionist's warm brown eyes. She was a plump older woman with a friendly, helpful demeanor, and I instantly got the feeling that there was something she didn't want to tell me.

"I'll buzz Officer Hamby and let him know you're here," she said, wrinkling her nose and holding up a finger.

For a moment, I just stared. Why did she need to buzz the cute policeman? Why couldn't she just go get Gran and tell her I was here to pick her up? Moreover, why wasn't Gran seated out in the waiting area with the other small-town hooligans?

I glanced down the narrow hallway to my left, which had a battered bulletin board plastered with lost-pet notices and missing-persons reports. I recognized the first room on the left as the bullpen. Several beat-up metal desks were scattered around, and I could hear phones ringing and keyboards clacking.

I looked from the receptionist to the bullpen and back to the receptionist, impatience and panic bubbling in my gut. She was speaking in low tones to someone on the other end of the line — someone I suspected was merely in the other room.

"Okay . . . all right. I'll send her in." The receptionist hung up the phone and turned her attention back to me.

"Officer Hamby is in an interview, but Detective Pierce can see you now." She gestured toward the bullpen.

I pulled a tight smile and strode across the waiting area, prepared to give someone a piece of my mind. Gran had been strangely tight-lipped about why she needed a lawyer, but I'd called R.P. Stein's office and left an urgent message with his secretary.

Was Gran in some kind of legal trouble? I knew she couldn't have gotten picked up for driving on a revoked license, because I'd had the Pinto all morning. I'd only been gone for a couple of hours. How much trouble could a ninety-two-year-old woman get into?

The bullpen smelled like old pizza and donuts, and I saw a tired-looking man striding toward me. He had light-brown hair that stuck up in the back, and he was wearing a wrinkled white button-up with slacks that looked as though they'd been slept in. He couldn't have been much older than Officer Hamby, but he had the sort of world-weary expression of a veteran cop who'd seen things he couldn't unsee.

"Miss McCrithers?"

"That's me."

"Detective Pierce. Officer Hamby is my partner. You're Virginia McCrithers's granddaughter, right?"

"Yeah." I glanced over the detective's shoulder, as if he might have stowed Gran over by the coffeemaker or something. "What's going on?"

Detective Pierce looked away and ran a hand through his already-disheveled hair. I got the feeling he did that a lot. "We brought your grandmother in to ask her a few questions regarding the death of Jay Mathers."

I stared at the detective for a long moment, not sure I'd

heard him correctly. "Jay Mathers? Wait, *why*? She wasn't even there. I mean, she was there, but she didn't actually see him die."

Detective Pierce sighed and braced his hands on his hips. "Were you aware that Jay Mathers had purchased the tax lien on your great-aunt's property?"

"The Mountain Shadow Grand? Yeah, I'm aware. I just inherited the place."

This seemed to be news to Detective Pierce. "*You* inherited it?"

"Yeah." I crossed my arms over my chest and set my jaw. *Geez.* These small-town cops were really light on the research. "If this is about the lien, don't you think you should be questioning *me*?"

The detective frowned. "Is there something you'd like to tell me?"

I rolled my eyes. "I don't know. You're the police. You still haven't told me what's going on."

Rather than taking offense, a worried look flashed across the detective's face, and he let out a heavy sigh. "Maybe we should talk in private."

He jerked his head back toward the hallway, and I followed him out of the bustling bullpen into a tiny room across the hall. This room had the same hideous wood paneling as the reception area and was bare, apart from a desk, two chairs, and a camera that was mounted to the wall.

Detective Pierce held out a hand, inviting me to sit, and it dawned on me then that this was an interrogation room. I'd only seen this kind of place in movies and TV shows, and I wondered if I should wait to say anything until R.P. arrived.

Cautiously, I took a seat, and Detective Pierce perched on the edge of the table. "What do you know about Jay Mathers and his . . . *activities* in this town?"

I shook my head. "Not much. Gran said he was some sort of developer, and my contractor just told me that he had plans to tear down The Mountain Shadow Grand and put in some condos . . . or maybe a mixed-use building."

The detective nodded as if this made sense and then fell into thoughtful silence. "Look, there's no easy way to say this, but . . . we have reason to believe that Jay Mathers might not have died of natural causes."

"What do you mean?" Surely the detective wasn't suggesting what it sounded as though he were saying.

"I mean, we're treating this as a possible homicide."

"You think this Mathers guy was *murdered*?" My stomach twisted as I thought back to that morning — the way he'd staggered out of the vehicle and the pained look on his face. I shook my head. "I-I thought maybe he choked or something."

Detective Pierce shook his head.

"A-and you think Gran might know something that could help you find the killer?" That seemed like a bit of a stretch, considering Gran only seemed to know what she'd picked up from the local rumor mill.

"We're exploring every possibility."

Something about the careful way he phrased his answer made my ears perk up.

"Are you staying with your grandmother while you're in town?"

I nodded. Why would he be asking that? Unless . . .

"Wait. You don't think —" I couldn't even bring myself to finish the sentence. It was too ridiculous for words.

"Do you know where your grandmother was Friday morning between seven and eight o'clock?"

Friday . . . Friday. I wracked my brain. Friday was the day that Mathers had died.

"Yeah, I —" I faltered when I remembered that Gran hadn't been at home when I'd woken up that morning. What time *was* that? I'd gotten up later than I'd intended, and it had been warm and sunny when I'd left. "I must have woken up around seven forty-five," I said, thinking out loud.

"And where was your grandmother?"

I shook my head, trying to remember if she'd told me where she'd gone. "She'd just baked some cookies when I woke up," I said. "So she couldn't have been gone that long."

"But she wasn't at home at the time?"

"No, I . . . I ran into her just after Mr. Mathers collapsed. She'd taken the dog for a walk around the neighborhood. She likes to exercise in the morning."

Detective Pierce nodded. "But, just to clarify, you are unaware of your grandmother's exact whereabouts between seven and eight."

I opened my mouth and closed it again, wishing I'd just told him she'd been at home with me. "You can't *seriously* think my gran had anything to do with Mathers's death?"

The detective raised an eyebrow but didn't meet my gaze. "Like I said, we're exploring every possibility."

I let out a bark of incredulous laughter. "She's ninety-two years old!"

"As I'm sure your grandmother would agree, age is just a number."

"And how do you think she killed him? Boring him to death with old *Leave It to Beaver* reruns?"

Detective Pierce's mouth became a hard line, though something in the set of his jaw told me he was trying not to laugh. "We're searching your grandmother's house as we speak."

That got my dander up. "And just what *exactly* are you hoping to find? The candlestick in the dining room or the lead pipe in the ballroom?" I rolled my eyes. "Better check Colonel Mustard's house next door while you're at it."

"I wouldn't joke about this if I were you," the detective said quietly. "We're taking this very seriously."

At that moment, someone walked past the room where we were speaking. I didn't see his face through the little plexiglass window at the top of the door, but something about the proud set of his shoulders told me it was Officer Hamby.

"Excuse me," I muttered, not caring if it was rude to walk out in the middle of an interrogation. I stuck my head out the door and called out Hamby's name. It came out much louder than I'd intended, and a mustachioed policeman halfway to the bullpen turned to look in my direction. The tall muscular officer with the military haircut did not.

Fuming, I strode down the hallway after him and tapped him on the shoulder — hard. Officer Handsome turned slowly on the spot, and I didn't think I was mistaking the look of dread in his eyes.

I crossed my arms over my chest and jerked my chin up in defiance. "Do you mind telling me why you've detained my grandmother in relation to Jay Mathers's death?"

I hadn't meant to bring my angry-mom posture to this conversation, but that was how I was standing.

Officer Hamby glanced over my shoulder at his partner, and something like a plea flashed through his eyes. When Detective Pierce didn't jump in, Hamby pressed his lips together. "The medical examiner says it looks as though Jay Mathers was poisoned."

Poisoned? That was possibly the last thing I'd expected to hear, though it did explain the choking and the pained look on his face.

"We have reason to believe someone slipped Mr. Mathers some strychnine."

"So?"

"*So*, Mathers's assistant claims your grandmother went to see him the morning he died."

I faltered. That was news to me. "That doesn't prove anything," I said breezily.

"She also says he and your grandmother argued," Hamby continued. "Do you have any idea what they might have been arguing about?"

"How should I know?"

Officer Hamby glanced back at his partner.

"She says she knew about the tax lien," Detective Pierce told him. "Apparently, Lucille Blackthorne left the hotel to her."

Officer Hamby raised his eyebrows before turning back to me. "And I suppose you realize that you won't be able to officially take possession of the property until the lien is redeemed?"

I blinked up at him in surprise but quickly schooled my expression.

"Public records show that the lien was set to expire in

less than a month," the detective continued. "At which time Mr. Mathers would have been within his rights to request the title to that property."

"But Gran was going to pay the tax lien," I said.

"Is that what she told you?"

I glared at Hamby, taken aback. "What are you implying?"

"I think there's something you should see."

Officer Hamby beckoned me into the bullpen, and I followed — not even taking the opportunity to check out his butt. That's how angry I was.

He led me over to a desk by the window, which was crowded with several gray plastic bins. "This is what we've recovered from your grandmother's place so far." He reached into one of the bins and grabbed a big plastic bag with lots of writing along the side and held it up for my inspection.

Inside was a bright-red box with the words "RAT B GONE" emblazoned across the front in huge black letters. "We found this under your grandmother's sink."

I stared dumbly at the box of rat poison, unsure why this was supposed to matter. That box had been under her kitchen sink for as long as I could remember.

"Strychnine was outlawed for use in indoor pesticides in nineteen eighty-nine," Hamby continued. "This rat poison was manufactured in nineteen eighty-two."

"So?" I spluttered, though I could see where Officer Hamby was going with this. "Gran has a value pack of toothpaste in her guest bathroom that's probably from the seventies."

Officer Hamby didn't laugh.

"You *really* think my ninety-two-year-old grandmother poisoned Jay Mathers?"

Officer Hamby shrugged. "High levels of strychnine can kill a person within minutes, though it can take as long as an hour. Jay Mathers's assistant came into work just as your grandmother was leaving, but she couldn't remember exactly what time that was. So unless your grandmother has an alibi for Friday morning between seven and eight o'clock —"

"I already told your partner. She was out walking."

Hamby just shook his head. "We haven't found anyone who's been able to confirm that. A few shop owners saw her walking along Main Street right around the time Mathers collapsed, but nobody claims to have seen her before that."

I let out an exasperated huff. There *had* to be witnesses. Hamby just hadn't tried very hard to find them because he wanted to solve this case. "Can I see her?"

Hamby glanced at his partner. I followed his gaze to Detective Pierce, who tilted his head in a way that seemed to say, "Lighten up."

Hamby gave a curt nod and led me back out of the bullpen, down to the very end of the hall. He stopped in front of another interrogation room and fished for a key hanging from his belt.

"You *locked her in*?" I said incredulously.

Officer Hamby wouldn't meet my gaze.

"I guess she *is* wearing her Skechers," I grumbled. "She might make a run for it."

Gran was seated primly in one of the hard metal chairs, her hands clasped in her lap. Snowball was sniffing the edge of the wall where it met the floor, his collar tinkling merrily. Gran perked up as I walked in, but I had a split second to see just how small and scared she looked sitting in that cold, empty room.

Snowball immediately ran up to greet me, jumping up on my leg.

"Snowball! Get down!" Gran scolded. "Caroline! What are you doing here?"

"I came to bail you out."

"And pull me away from this handsome policeman?" Gran shot Hamby a lascivious look. "We were really hitting it off."

"Gran . . ." I sat down in the chair across from her and lowered my voice to a serious tone. "The police need to know where you were Friday morning between seven and eight o'clock."

"I already told them. Snowball and I went out for a walk. You know, I still get around pretty good for my age."

"I know you do, Gran, but . . ." I grimaced. "Jay Mathers's assistant says you went by his office Friday morning."

"Oh, she *did*, did she?" Gran rolled her eyes.

I waited. "And did you?"

Gran scoffed. "Caroline, my memory's still pretty sharp, but I can't be expected to remember *everywhere* I went last week. What does any of this have to do with anything?"

"They think you poisoned Jay Mathers."

"That's ridiculous." Gran frowned at me as though this were somehow my fault. "Where's R.P.?"

"I called him on my way over. Let's get you home and let him sort this out." I threw Officer Hamby a withering look and reached out to help Gran to her feet.

"Uh . . ." Officer Hamby cleared his throat. "I'm afraid that's not going to be possible. I . . . can't let your grandmother leave."

I turned to glare at him, steam coming out of my ears. What was *with* this guy?

"*Ooh!*" said Gran, looking suddenly excited. "The plot thickens."

Officer Hamby threw her the sort of look a teacher might give a student for talking out of turn, squared his shoulders, and drew in a breath. "Virginia McCrithers, you're under arrest for the murder of Jay Mathers."

CHAPTER NINE

After a long talk with Gran's attorney, I found myself at a dead end. Apparently, the rat poison, the tax lien, and the assistant's statement that Gran had been at Mathers's office was all the police felt they needed to hold her.

R.P. couldn't bail Gran out until she'd been arraigned, so I hit the streets to find *someone* who'd seen her out walking the morning Jay Mathers had died. The trouble was that most of the shops on Main Street didn't open until nine, and any weekend tourists who might have seen Gran on Friday morning were likely long gone by Monday.

Two hours into our search, Snowball had lain down in the middle of the sidewalk and refused to go any farther. I'd dropped him and Desmond off at Gran's and doubled back to continue the mission.

By four o'clock, my feet were killing me, and I hadn't had anything to eat since breakfast. The glowing neon sign of the divey-looking bar next to the tearoom caught my eye, and I staggered in to down a nice stiff drink and eat my weight in whatever greasy food they were serving.

Chumley's was a dim, dingy place with spotted mirrors and tufted leather booths all along one wall. The polished oak bar was deserted, apart from a man in a black bomber jacket, who sat slumped at the very end. Moody jazz music was playing over the loudspeaker as a surly-looking bartender dried pint glasses with a rag.

"We're closed," he called, not bothering to look up from his task.

I froze just inside the doorway, my feet barking at the thought of walking even one more block to reach the next sad watering hole.

"We open at five. Come back then."

"What about him?" I asked, pointing at the man, who may or may not have been snoring.

"Oh." The bartender shook his head. "Reggie doesn't count. He's been here since last night."

"*Please*?" I groaned, throwing my head back and not caring that I sounded desperate. "You don't even have to dirty a glass. I'm gonna need the whole bottle."

The man froze with a glass in hand and raised one dark eyebrow. "Rough day?"

"The worst."

He stared at me for a long moment and then let out his breath in a huff. "All right," he said. "What's your poison?"

"Gin," I said, sliding gratefully onto the nearest barstool.

"Gin and —"

"Just gin."

Looking vaguely concerned for my safety, the man

produced a bottle of Tanqueray and poured two fingers into a glass. I guessed that demanding the whole bottle wasn't really a thing.

As he poured, I couldn't help noticing the enticing way his tattooed biceps bulged from the sleeves of his tight black T-shirt.

Nope. Since the whole ordeal with Todd, I'd sworn off men. I clearly couldn't trust my instincts.

I forced myself to look away from the yummy bartender, and as I did, my gaze snagged on five little wooden plaques hanging behind the bar that read *Employee of the Month*. Each one bore the picture of the scowling bartender with the name Gideon Brewer etched beneath.

"Employee of the month, huh?"

Gideon rolled his eyes. "I'm the *only* employee." He waved the bottle of gin toward the plaques. "The owner just does that to irritate me."

"Huh."

I took a sip from the glass he slid my way and drummed my fingers on the bar top. Drinking one's sorrows with only the company of the bartender was a lot more awkward than they made it look in the movies.

As my eyes searched for something half as enticing as Gideon's muscles to settle on, I spotted a stack of laminated menus near the end of the bar. The words "bacon-wrapped jalapeños stuffed with cream cheese" seemed to jump off the page, and my mouth immediately began to water. They didn't exactly conform to the standards of my special anti-inflammatory diet, but it had been a rough day.

"Could I get an order of jalapeño poppers?" I asked,

thinking I might be able to sweet-talk my way into it, since I'd gotten him to pour me a drink.

"Kitchen opens at five."

My heart sank, and I let out a heavy sigh. "It's not good to drink on an empty stomach."

Gideon shot me a "don't push your luck" kind of look and shoved a little bowl of pretzels at me. I wrinkled my nose at the half-empty bowl of broken pretzels that were clearly from the night before, but I was so hungry that I gingerly plucked one out of the bowl and popped it into my mouth.

Gideon drifted off to check on the glassy-eyed regular at the other end of the bar, and I pulled my day planner out of my purse and flipped to a clean page. Since I'd struck out on finding a witness to account for Gran's whereabouts, I needed to record everything I'd learned so far, in the hope that something might jump out at me.

I started by jotting down what I knew of the murder timeline — if, in fact, Mathers *had* been murdered.

7:00-8:00 a.m. — Victim poisoned?

8ish — Me leave house

8:15 — Approx. time of death

"What's so bad it's driving you to drink and journal?" came Gideon's low, rumbly voice.

I looked up to find him staring at me from behind the bar, and he nodded down at my Filofax. "It's not a journal. It's a planner," I said, my voice coming out sounding a little more defensive than I'd meant for it to. "And I'm taking notes about the murder of Jay Mathers."

"*Murder?*" Gideon's eyebrows scrunched together. "Why do they think he was murdered?"

"No idea. But apparently the police think he was

poisoned — with strychnine." Biting on the inside of my cheek, I bent my head and jotted that down, too.

Gideon eyed me warily. "You a reporter or something?"

"No," I sighed, setting down my pen and staring at my meager notes. "The police brought my grandmother in for questioning, and now they've arrested her in connection with his murder. I need to figure out what *really* happened so I can get her off the hook."

"Who's your grandma?"

"Ginger McCrithers."

As I said her name, a look of recognition flashed across Gideon's face, and his right eye twitched in what could have been a wink or possibly a grimace. "This may be an insensitive question, but . . . are you sure your gran didn't do it?"

"What? Yes, of course I'm sure! She's, like, a billion years old, and she had her dog with her at the time. I seriously doubt she would have brought her *dog* to do a murder!"

"To *do* a murder?" Gideon's bottom lip curled in amusement. "You sure you're up for this, Nancy Drew?"

"No. I just spent the last four hours traipsing up and down Main Street trying to find a witness that could give Gran an alibi, but no cigar."

Gideon frowned. "Are we talking about the same person?" He brought his hand level with his pecs. "About four foot eleven, white hair, wears those hideous tracksuits when she walks her little white dog?"

"Yeah, that's her," I said slowly. "Why?"

Gideon shook his head. "No reason. It's just . . . you

would think someone would have remembered seeing her."

"You would think," I sighed, slumping against the bar in defeat.

Gideon was right. I was no detective. If the police couldn't find a suspect better than Gran, why did I think I'd be able to get to the bottom of this?

"Not saying your gran did it, but she could be pretty scary," Gideon continued. "One time I made the mistake of 'parking in her spot' at the hardware store, and . . ." He shook his head and let out a low whistle. "Let's just say I wouldn't be all that shocked if someone told me she'd killed Mathers."

"Thanks a lot."

He grinned. "Then again, Mathers had a lot of enemies."

"Anyone in particular I should be looking at?"

"How much time you got?"

I raised my eyebrows, silently urging him to continue, and Gideon let out a sigh. "Mathers made his living tearing down old historic buildings and slapping up pricey apartments that he could turn a quick profit on. He actually just bought this building." Gideon gestured around him.

I hurriedly made a note in my planner. That explained why he'd wanted to acquire the hotel. It was right across the street.

"Anyway, I guess he was going to tear it down and put a six-story mixed-use building with businesses on the first floor and apartments up above. When he first submitted the plans, it was only for a three-story building. People weren't happy about it, given his reputation, but the town council approved. Then he resubmitted the plans with three more stories added. Well, when *The Gazette* got ahold of that . . ." Gideon shook his head. "Half the town was up in arms about it, but in the end he won. A lot of people will be happy to see Jay Mathers dead."

"What's going to happen to the building now?"

Gideon shrugged. "Who knows? Mathers was married and had two adult children — neither of whom seemed to have followed in his footsteps. My guess is they'll either sell the building or leave it as-is and continue to collect rent from the existing tenants."

I considered that for a moment. A towering six-story structure would completely change the look of downtown — not just Phantom Canyon Boulevard. The Mountain Shadow Grand would no longer be the dominant feature, and a huge development would have thrown the other little shops and restaurants into shadow. I could understand why people had been angry, particularly if he'd planned on building six stories all along and had only held back to gain initial approval.

Jay Mathers had duped the whole town.

Suddenly, all those feelings I'd had after I'd learned Todd had scammed me came rushing back at once. My stomach twisted into painful knots, and my ears began to ring.

Then came that out-of-control panicky feeling that the rug had been pulled out from under me. My chest constricted, and my breathing became shallow. I gripped the edge of the bar tighter.

"You all right?" Gideon asked.

I looked up to find him watching me carefully, as if he was afraid I might throw up.

"Fine," I lied, raising my glass with a shaky hand and taking a huge swig of gin.

I wasn't fine, but I would have to be. I couldn't allow myself to spiral. I had to figure out who was responsible for Jay Mathers's death so Gran wouldn't be forced to live out her final years in some scary women's prison.

"I'll go put in those jalapeño poppers," said Gideon, still watching me with concern. "You look like you could use another drink, and I don't want to have to carry you out of here."

CHAPTER TEN

Climbing unsteadily out of the Pinto, I had to fight the roiling nausea and the nasty hungover ache in my muscles. Three drinks with Gideon had left me with a splitting headache and an inability to keep anything down, apart from a couple of stale ginger cookies.

Gran's arraignment hearing was being held at the Fourth Judicial District Court down in Colorado Springs. R.P. had requested the opportunity to meet with Gran before the hearing, and he looked as though he were there for a funeral rather than a simple arraignment. Gran was still wearing her same ruby velour tracksuit from the day before, and she looked more tired than I'd ever seen her.

"Are you all right?" I asked.

"Fine," she said in a dismissive voice, drawing herself up to her full height and fluffing her cloud of white hair. "Just a little stiff from sleeping on that infernal cot they gave me. I'm not thirty years old anymore, you know."

My stomach clenched when I thought about Gran having to spend the night in jail. Right then, I made a promise to myself that she would never have to do that again.

"I have some news," said R.P. in a hushed tone. His hands shook slightly as he pulled a folder out of his worn leather briefcase and opened it to a report. "They got the results back on a plate of cookies found in Mathers's office." R.P. sighed and glanced at Gran. "The lab found traces of strychnine present."

Something like dread flashed across Gran's face, but I was still confused. "Wait. What does that have to do with Gran?"

R.P. was still looking at her as he said, "Your prints were all over the plate the poisoned cookies came on."

"*What?*" My heart skipped a beat, and I rounded on Gran. "Why would your fingerprints be on that plate?"

"I may have brought Mr. Mathers cookies to sweeten him up," Gran grumbled. "But I didn't *poison* them."

I turned to R.P. "And they're *sure* there was strychnine in the cookies?"

He nodded. "The cookies were sent off to a lab for independent testing. There was strychnine in the cookies themselves and on the plate they came on."

"But that doesn't make any sense!" I cried. "I ate two of those leftover cookies this morning!"

I glanced at Gran, who looked just as worried and confused as I felt.

R.P. frowned at his client. "And these were the same cookies you brought Jay Mathers?"

"The cookies in the kitchen are the ones I brought Mathers, but again, I didn't poison them."

"Why were you bringing this developer guy cookies?" I asked. "And why were you there in the first place?"

"That's my business, Caroline. But if you *must* know, I went over there to gloat."

"To *gloat*?"

Gran nodded. "That snake-in-the-grass Mathers has been trying to get his slimy hands on Lucille's hotel for years. I wanted to be the first to tell him that he'd wasted his time."

I narrowed my eyes at her. "So you brought him *cookies*?"

Gran shrugged. "I thought it might help soften the blow."

"The toxicology report on the body will tell us more, but unfortunately it isn't in yet," said R.P. "That could take weeks — months, even — but the medical examiner felt confident in the cause of death. The hallmarks of strychnine poisoning are very distinctive, and the cookies were all he had in his stomach at the time."

"Is there a photo of the cookies they found at the scene?" I spluttered. I felt certain that Gran hadn't tried to kill Jay Mathers, and the fact that I was still standing proved she hadn't gone senile and accidentally mixed rat poison in with the dough. Maybe someone had switched out Gran's cookies for the poisoned ones in an attempt to set her up?

R.P. bent down and heaved his briefcase onto the table between us. He rifled through a stack of folders and produced a thick sheath of papers. His brown furrowed as he leafed through them, finally producing an eight-by-ten photo that showed a paper plate printed with dancing snowmen and four uneaten ginger cookies.

My heart sank. I recognized those plates. They were the

same ones Gran had kept in her cupboard for the last ten years.

"Those aren't my cookies," said Gran with an edge of annoyance.

"But those are your plates," I pointed out.

"So what? They aren't my cookies. There's too much sugar on top." She pointed at the photograph and then looked up at R.P. "I use mostly molasses for sweetening."

Staring at the photo, I could see what Gran was talking about. Little granules of sugar gleamed all around the outer surface of the cookies. The granules were larger and less refined than ordinary table sugar, though I couldn't say if there was more than she usually rolled the dough in.

"Could I get a copy of these photos?" I asked.

R.P. nodded, and the lines across his brow seemed to deepen. "I'm afraid the mere appearance of the cookies and Caroline's testimony won't be enough to get this thrown out," he said quietly. "They have an eyewitness who says she saw you at Jay Mathers's office the morning he was killed. The police discovered rat poison containing strychnine at your house. And the cookies —" He shook his head. "The prosecution will argue that you had motive to kill Mathers, since he held the tax lien to your sister's property."

Something about R.P.'s tone intensified my dread. He didn't sound at all confident that he'd be able to get Gran off.

"Ginger," he said in a low voice. "I respect you too much to lie to you. This does not look good."

"Are you suggesting *I* poisoned him?" Gran scoffed.

"I'm not suggesting anything," said R.P., looking frustrated. "But you had motive, means, and opportunity." He lowered his voice and glanced at me. "Now, if there's something I should know about your mental state . . ." He trailed off hopefully. "I could argue that you are not competent to stand trial, or we could enter the plea of 'not guilty' due to dementia or cognitive impairment."

"Cognitive impairment?" Gran rounded on R.P. "Who do you think you're talking to?"

I winced. I could have told R.P. he was barking up the wrong tree suggesting Gran was going senile.

"I just thought I'd ask," he said, holding up his hands in mock surrender. "How would you like to plea?"

"Not guilty! I thought that should be obvious," Gran muttered, frowning at R.P. "And don't think I'm going to forget that you questioned my mental state. I may be old, but I haven't lost my mind just yet."

R.P. didn't smile or chuckle. His expression was deadly serious.

Fortunately, I didn't have time to panic. Within minutes, he was leading us into the cold, drab courtroom, where a woman in a navy pantsuit on the opposite side of the aisle was poring over pages of notes. The Colorado state flag and the American flag hung behind the judge's bench.

I helped Gran lower herself into one of the heavy wooden chairs and had barely taken a seat myself when the judge walked in. She was a large woman with dark skin and jet-black hair, which she wore in a twist at the base of her neck.

"All rise," the bailiff announced.

I scrambled to my feet and went over to help Gran. The judge's hawklike gaze swiveled over to land on us, but her expression gave nothing away.

"Be seated."

I was sure no one else heard Gran's scoff of irritation that she had to sit back down right after being asked to stand.

After the clerk had greeted everyone, the prosecuting attorney read the charges against Gran: murder in the first degree.

"Mr. Stein, have you discussed the charges with your client?" asked the judge.

"I have," said R.P.

"Mrs. McCrithers, do you understand the charges?"

"*Yes*," said Gran. Her answer was polite enough, but there was a definite edge of annoyance to her voice.

"Mrs. McCrithers, how do you plead?"

"Not guilty," said Gran, her voice ringing out in the courtroom with an air of finality.

"The defendant has entered a plea of 'not guilty.' Given the serious nature of the crime, I would normally ask the defendant to be held without bail until trial. However, given the defendant's age and her ties to the community, I do not believe that she is a flight risk."

In front of me, Gran's head wobbled, and I was certain she was rolling her eyes.

"Bail is set at one million dollars."

I sucked in a breath.

"Your honor," R.P. cut in. "We motion for Mrs. McCrithers to be released under her own recognizance."

"Objection." The prosecuting attorney got to her feet. "Your honor, the defendant has been charged with murder in the first degree. I'm extremely uncomfortable with the idea of her back on the streets."

"Your honor, my client is in her nineties," R.P. replied.

"She seldom has occasion to be roaming 'the streets.'" He cast the prosecuting attorney a sidelong look. "She has also suffered some health setbacks since the death of her sister, and her granddaughter has come to live with her until such a time that Mrs. McCrithers can arrange professional home care."

I raised my eyebrows. This was news to me. I couldn't imagine Gran would go for it. Although, if it was between acting a little decrepit and going to jail . . .

"Your honor, this is the first I'm hearing of this," said the prosecuting attorney in an exasperated tone.

"I just received a signed letter from her physician this morning," said R.P. smoothly, producing a piece of paper from the stack in front of him.

The judge nodded. "You may approach the bench."

R.P. hustled up to the bench to present the letter from Gran's doctor. "Your honor, if there are no objections, I'd like to request that my client be granted compassionate release. She should be allowed to await trial from the comfort of her own home, with electronic monitoring, where she can continue to receive care from her medical team." He paused for effect. "I would like to remind the court that this is her first offense."

The judge looked to the prosecuting attorney.

"I have no objections, your honor."

"Very well, then. The defendant will be placed under house arrest with electronic monitoring to await trial." The judge smacked the bench with her gavel. "Court is adjourned."

I got to my feet as the judge exited the courtroom, my knees shaking uncontrollably.

"A million dollars bail?" Gran groused, pushing herself up on the arms of the chair. "What am I, made of money?"

"Be glad your physician's assistant returns phone calls promptly," R.P. quipped, returning to his seat.

"Because *apparently*, I'm falling apart." Gran turned to me with a playful twinkle in her soft blue-green eyes. "Caroline, since you're now my live-in nurse, be a dear and rub my feet?"

"I don't know, Gran. That might disturb your flashy new ankle monitor."

Gran chuckled, but R.P. turned to me and gripped my arm with a surprising amount of force. "I'm sure I don't have to tell you how serious this is," he murmured. "Anyone who knows your grandmother knows she is *not* in ill health. It is very important that you stay with her until the trial, or this little arrangement could go up in smoke."

I swallowed and nodded as the bailiff came to take Gran. I didn't know how I was going to swing staying in Mountain Shadow indefinitely. I needed to get back to Chicago and hope I still had a job when I returned. But a live-in nurse sounded expensive, and I didn't think Gran would go for it anyway, so I would have to figure it out.

"I'll be in touch," said R.P., gathering his briefcase and preparing to leave.

"Mr. Stein —"

"Yes?"

I let out the breath I'd been holding and lowered my voice. "You don't really think there's a chance Gran could be convicted, do you? I mean, she obviously didn't *kill* the guy."

R.P. stopped in the process of organizing his papers

and drew in a deep breath. "Caroline, I wish I could tell you that they don't have a prayer in the world. I wish I could say their case was weak and that I could make this all go away. But . . ."

There was a long beat of silence. "*But?*"

R.P. sighed and glanced over his shoulder at Gran, who was being led away by the bailiff. "If I hadn't known your grandmother for years, I would say it looked as though she'd done it."

CHAPTER ELEVEN

After Gran was released, I brought her straight home — nervous about the flashing gray piece of plastic that was now strapped to her ankle. As soon as I got her settled in her favorite chair with *Law & Order* and a glass of chocolate milk, she promptly passed out.

I knew I wouldn't be able to sleep — not after R.P.'s chilling proclamation — and I still had a few hours to kill before my appointment with the elevator guy that afternoon.

I decided to pay a little visit to Jay Mathers's personal assistant, who'd seen Gran leaving his office the morning of his death. Officer Hamby seemed convinced that Gran was guilty of murder, and unless I could find another explanation for Mathers's death, I was afraid he might get a conviction.

It had started to rain by the time Desmond and I pulled up in front of the outdated red-brick building on the other end of Phantom Canyon Boulevard. The sky was an ominous pewter gray, and the temperature had dropped to a chilly fifty-two degrees.

Given cats' general hatred of rain and cold weather, I'd been surprised that Desmond had wanted to come with me rather than stay curled up on one of Gran's afghans. But after winding himself around my legs and tripping me repeatedly on my way out the door, I'd decided to bring him along.

"Wish me luck," I told him, shimmying into the khaki trench coat that Gran kept in the backseat of the Pinto. It was a little tight in the shoulders and only came down to my knees, but at least it would keep me dry.

Desmond blinked at me, and I slipped out of the car and hustled up the stairs to the second floor. Mathers's office was just across Main Street from the hotel, sandwiched between a realtor's office and a dentist. The spotless glass door had "Mathers Properties" etched across it in big bold letters, and the scent of drywall and fresh paint greeted me as I entered the sparse reception area.

A single midcentury armchair sat by the window, along with an obligatory potted plant. Blue painter's tape was stuck to the underside of the crown molding, as if the office was still being remodeled. That would explain the utter lack of personality and cold, corporate feel of the place.

A young woman with brown hair was seated at a desk, and just behind her hung a huge glass plaque that bore the same logo that was etched in the door. Her hair was done up in a neat chignon, and she wore a cream-colored turtleneck sweater to offset the chill of the aggressively air-conditioned building.

She looked up from her computer the moment I walked in, and I knew immediately that she'd been crying.

"Can I help you?" she asked, dabbing under her nose with a crumpled tissue.

"Uh . . . yeah." I glanced to the left at the closed office door, which was sealed with police tape and papered with notices about it being an active crime scene. There went any hope that I might be able to get a look inside Mr. Mathers's office.

I chewed for a moment on my bottom lip, trying to decide how to broach the topic. "You're Mr. Mathers's assistant, right?"

At the mention of her former boss, fresh tears welled up in the assistant's eyes. So much for the direct approach. "I-I was," she stammered. "My name's Monica."

I grimaced at my use of the present tense. "I'm so sorry for your loss."

"Thanks," she sniffled, dabbing under her eyes and trying to pull herself together. She glanced once at her computer screen before looking back at me. "H-how can I help you?"

I hesitated for another moment before deciding to just go with the truth. "Look, I'm really sorry to bother you right now, what with everything that's happened . . . but the police just arrested my grandmother in connection with Mr. Mathers's death, and I'd really like to understand what happened the morning he died."

Something flickered in Monica's expression, though I couldn't tell if it was guilt, suspicion, or anger.

"Obviously, my gran didn't *kill* Mr. Mathers."

I waited a beat to see how the young woman would react, but she just stared at me with those puffy red eyes.

I cleared my throat. "The detective mentioned that you'd seen my gran leaving the office sometime Friday morning?"

Monica's gaze flickered to the desk and then to the side, as though she were trying to recall the details. "Uh, yeah. I heard her and Jay arguing as I came up the stairs, though I couldn't make out what they were saying."

"Do you know what time that was?"

Monica swallowed. "I-I'm not sure. I usually get in around seven, but I was running late that morning. I think I got here around seven thirty or seven forty-five."

My heart sank. That was right around the time that Mathers had been poisoned and fell neatly into the window for which Gran was unaccounted for. If Monica *had* seen Gran leaving at that time, it would fit with the police's theory that she'd poisoned Mathers.

"How did Mr. Mathers seem to you after you saw my gran?" I asked. "Was he . . . *upset*?"

"I . . . didn't see Mr. Mathers the morning that he died," said Monica in a quiet voice.

I frowned. "Really?"

She shook her head. "Like I said, I came into work later than usual. I . . . overslept. Your grandmother was leaving just as I was coming up the stairs."

"And Mr. Mathers was in his office?" I pointed to the door with the police tape over it.

Monica nodded. "H-he jumped on a phone call right when I came in, and I didn't want to disturb him."

"Makes sense. But I saw him on Main Street around eight fifteen or so. He had to walk right past your desk."

"Yeah. I had to pick up some documents to take to the post office. He was already gone by the time I got back."

Her voice broke on the last few words, and she scrunched up her fingers under her nose.

"What time was that?" I felt bad about making her go through the details when she was clearly so upset, but I couldn't shake the feeling that there was something she wasn't telling me.

"Just before eight thirty." She sniffed.

"Do you have any idea where he was going?"

Monica opened her mouth, thinking hard. "I expect he was on his way to his nine o'clock appointment in Colorado Springs. He was meeting with his attorney."

"Business?"

Monica swallowed and shook her head. "A divorce attorney."

A-ha.

"So . . . you handle his schedule?"

"I'm his assistant," she said, a little defensively. "It's my job."

"Right. Of course," I said, deciding not to press the issue. I figured I'd get more information out of her if she didn't sense that I was making any judgments or accusations.

"What was it like, working for Mr. Mathers?" I knew I was pushing my luck asking such a leading question, but I was desperate for any morsel of information that might give me insight into his murder.

Suspicion flickered in Monica's eyes, and I saw immediately when her walls went up. "Why are you asking?"

"Just wondering," I said in what I hoped passed for a casual tone.

"Were you wondering if *I* had some motive to kill my

boss?" she snapped, any pretense of friendliness evaporating at once.

"No, I —"

"Jay was a good man," she cut in. "He wasn't *perfect*, but no one is. He worked harder than anyone I've ever met, and he did a lot for this community."

Like buying up historic buildings to tear down? I thought.

"I'm sorry," I said. "I didn't mean to pry. And I wasn't implying you had anything to do with this. I'm just desperate to find something the police might have overlooked so that I can clear my grandmother's name. She can be a bit prickly when she wants to be, but she's a sweet person. She didn't do this."

Monica blinked, and her expression softened, as if taken aback by my honesty. I could practically see her claws retracting as she said, "If it makes you feel any better, I don't think your grandmother did this either."

"You don't?"

She shook her head. "I've seen her a few times before . . . at the community development meetings. She is . . . *prickly*, but she seems harmless."

I nodded. I could imagine what Gran had been like at those meetings, and "prickly" was probably an understatement. "Can you think of anyone who'd want to see Mr. Mathers dead?"

Monica raised both eyebrows, opened her mouth, and then closed it again. "Speaking *generally*?"

I nodded to encourage her to continue.

"Jay pretty much always had a target on his back. That's typical for development projects." She let out a little puff of air. Then a far-off look came over her, and she sat up a little straighter. "You should look into Bellamy Broussard," she said, speaking low and fast as if we might be overheard. "He was one of the most outspoken opponents on the Phantom Canyon Boulevard project."

I squinted. "The building with the bar?"

Monica nodded. "Mr. Broussard went to the mat to derail that project. He petitioned the town council to get the building designated as a local landmark, which — according to town ordinances — would make any proposed changes to the site subject to review by the Mountain Shadow historical society."

At this point, I was sort of following her train of thought, but I wanted her to spell it out for me. "Meaning . . ."

"*Meaning* we would have to stay true to the original design of the building. It would have completely derailed the project. Mr. Broussard knew that, of course." Monica rolled her eyes.

"Did he have some kind of vendetta against Mr. Mathers, or did he just want to prevent that building from being developed?"

Monica looked thoughtful. "I think he was still upset about Jay getting the tax lien for The Mountain Shadow Grand."

At the mention of the hotel, my ears perked up. "Why is that? Did Mr. Broussard have some interest in the property?"

Monica nodded. "Bellamy Broussard owns The Wind Chime Inn Bed and Breakfast. He tried to buy your aunt's place a few years back when she first lapsed on her property taxes, but he lost out to Jay on the auction for the tax lien." Monica narrowed her eyes and tapped a finger on her lips. "Bellamy Broussard is *such* a busybody. I'll bet you anything he heard about your aunt's death and didn't want to take any chances."

I considered her theory for a moment. "But if that's true — if he *did* know Lucille was dead — he must have known that her estate would pay to redeem the tax lien."

"I'm not sure he would take that chance," said Monica. "Bellamy Broussard is a shark. If Jay had had the opportunity to secure the title for the property, he could have turned around and built a modern five-star hotel that would wipe out Mr. Broussard's little B&B." She leaned forward, holding me rooted to the spot with her big bloodshot eyes. "I think Mr. Broussard saw Jay as a threat to his business."

CHAPTER TWELVE

After a quick stop at Déjà Brew, Desmond and I pulled up along the curb in front of The Wind Chime Inn. The bed and breakfast was situated on a quiet street in an old Victorian home painted a delicate shade of blue.

The house had a huge wrap-around porch lined with slat-back rockers. The garden was bursting with neatly trimmed rose bushes, and the whole property was hemmed in by a white picket fence. "Idyllic" was the word that sprang to mind, and I had a hard time believing that the adorable B&B was owned by a cold-blooded killer.

"What do you think, Des?" I asked around a mouthful of tuna salad. In addition to making the perfect mocha, my favorite new coffee shop also served a variety of delectable sandwiches on gluten-free bread.

Desmond leaned over, bracing his paws on my leg, his nose twitching toward my sandwich. A big hunk of tuna salad fell out of the bottom onto the brown paper bag I was using as a napkin, and I plucked it up and held it out for him. Des snatched it delicately out of my fingers, his yellow eyes bulging with gluttonous delight as he noshed.

A quick online search showed that Bellamy Broussard had purchased The Wind Chime Inn two years earlier. There was no way to verify the assistant's claim that he'd tried to buy The Grand, but if he was trying to monopolize Mountain Shadow's hospitality industry, it wouldn't be strange for him to try to purchase the old hotel.

Polishing off my sandwich, I washed it down with a sip of my latte and left Desmond to scrounge in the paper sack for any tuna morsels I might have missed. We'd gotten a brief reprieve from the rain, though the world still smelled like wet pavement and earth. Wind chimes tinkled musically as I made my way up the front walkway and let myself in the front door.

The parlor of The Wind Chime Inn looked as though it had been decorated by someone's grandma in the late eighteen hundreds. A fussy little antique settee and several tufted pastel chairs were crowded into the seating area by the front desk, and a silver tea service gleamed by the window. Lace doilies covered nearly every available surface, accenting vases of dried flowers, brass music boxes, ceramic figurines, and other old-lady paraphernalia.

"Good afternoon!" came an upbeat, friendly voice.

I jumped and looked around. The voice seemed to have originated from a huge potted fern in the far corner, but then a dark head of hair appeared in the foliage.

A good-looking man stepped out to greet me, a giant feather duster in hand. It was an odd fit, given his wardrobe. He wore a pair of pressed charcoal slacks and a lilac shirt set off with a loud paisley tie. His jet-black hair was gelled in a rather severe style that made it look permanently windblown.

He hurriedly tucked the feather duster behind his back, as though I'd caught him doing something undignified. "Can I help you?" he asked. His voice was prim and polite but utterly businesslike — sort of like a snooty English butler.

"Uh —" I hesitated, taken aback by his sudden entrance. "I'm looking for the owner . . . Mr. Broussard?"

The man's eyes flashed, and he stood up a little straighter. "Please. Call me Bellamy."

"Oh! N-nice to meet you." I wasn't sure why I was so surprised that the man before me was Bellamy Broussard. I supposed I'd been expecting someone older, but Bellamy looked to be in his early to midthirties.

"Sorry, I just . . ." I trailed off, trying to gather my thoughts. Clearly, my talk with Monica hadn't done much to improve my interrogation skills. I cleared my throat and extended a hand. "My name is Caroline McCrithers. Lucille Blackthorne was my great-aunt."

Bellamy took my hand and lifted one dark eyebrow. Despite its masculine thickness, I could tell by its shapely arch that it was very intentionally groomed. "You're the new owner of The Mountain Shadow Grand."

"I am. Well, I will be, just as soon as we get a few legal matters ironed out." I quickly withdrew my hand from his, opening and closing my palms. Why had I felt the need to add that caveat? Given that Bellamy had tried to purchase the hotel from Aunt Lucille and later the tax lien on the property, he must have known that the hotel was in financial trouble.

"I'm . . . sorry for your loss," he said stiffly.

"Thank you." I cleared my throat and stuffed my hands into the pockets of Gran's coat. What was it about Bellamy Broussard that made me terrified of saying the wrong thing?

He lifted both eyebrows expectantly and started moving across the room. "How can I help?" he asked, busily straightening vases and fluffing pillows as if to say he didn't really have the time to talk to me. "That property needs a lot of work. It's not a project for the faint of heart." He turned to me and arched an eyebrow. "Or the inexperienced."

I stiffened at that little dig, certain it had been intentional. Bellamy was still buzzing around the parlor like an industrious maid, fussing with the plants and straightening furniture.

"It's . . . keeping me busy," I allowed. Or it *would* have been, if I weren't trying to track down Jay Mathers's true killer. "I was wondering if I could . . . ask you a few questions."

"About the hotel?" Bellamy paused in his obsessive tidying, and I knew I had his attention.

"Uh, sort of." I pressed my lips together, unsure how to proceed. "I'm new in town, but Jay Mathers's assistant Monica mentioned that you once tried to purchase the hotel."

"I did." Bellamy turned his back to me once again, dusting the mahogany secretary desk that sat along the wall opposite the window.

"Could you tell me what happened?"

"There really isn't much to tell. I was interested in the hotel at the time, and I saw that Lucille had fallen behind on her property taxes." He picked up a vase of dried roses and turned toward me with a carefully somber expression in place. "I'd heard she'd recently moved into a nursing facility down in the Springs, and I knew the hotel must be causing some financial strain." He shrugged and set the roses back down, picking up the feather duster and tickling the brittle blooms. "I offered to purchase the hotel, but Lucille didn't want to sell."

That all sounded reasonable — if a bit opportunistic — but it didn't tell me anything I didn't already know. "If you don't mind me asking . . . what was your interest in The Grand?"

"What's anyone's interest in Colorado real estate?" Bellamy asked with a smirk. "Not to be crass, but property values in this town have skyrocketed over the last ten years. I hadn't yet purchased this place, and I wanted the hotel as an investment."

"Uh-huh . . ."

"Why? Are you selling?" In an instant, Bellamy's whole demeanor seemed to change, and he pivoted toward me with an eager expression.

"No," I said. "It was Aunt Lucille's dying wish that I restore the hotel, and right now that's the plan."

"Well, I hope you're independently wealthy," said Bellamy with a scoff, his gaze drifting over my borrowed coat and the scuffed toes of my suede flats. "That place needs a *lot* of work, and the contractors specializing in commercial renovations are the biggest con artists you can imagine. I would *hate* to see you get taken for a ride."

That little comment felt like a personal attack, but I took a deep breath and reminded myself that Bellamy couldn't possibly know about what had happened with Todd.

"Nope," I said brightly, trying to let it slide off my back. "I'm definitely not what you think of when you hear the word 'heiress,' but I'll find a way to make it work."

The words came out sounding much more confident than I felt, but Bellamy didn't look fooled. "Mmhmm."

I licked my lips and shifted my weight from one foot to the other, gearing up to ask the questions I'd come to get answers to. "I'm sure you know that Jay Mathers held the certificates for the tax liens . . ."

"Yes," said Bellamy. "I heard he had big plans for that place."

His tone was light and breezy, but there was a harsh edge to the words that made me think there *had* been bad blood between him and Mathers.

"What sort of plans?"

"He wanted to tear the whole thing down and slap up a bunch of hideous condos."

"Is that what he planned to do with the building across the street?" I asked.

"No. He was going to turn that into some mixed-use building. He thought he could pull the wool over everyone's eyes when he first submitted the plans for a three-story structure. Then he resubmits the plans, and all of a sudden it's six stories?"

"Is that why you petitioned the town council to get the building designated as a local landmark?"

Bellamy snorted. "You should have *seen* Mathers when he came to confront me," he said in a confidential, gossipy tone. "He'd probably been giddy when Gladys Hutchins sold him that building. He thought he was going to be making money hand over fist!"

I waited in silence, holding my breath. I felt as though

I'd just cracked Bellamy's dignified, sophisticated outer shell, and I had the faint hope that he might let his guard down entirely and tell me everything I wanted to know.

"It was the right thing to do," Bellamy added, almost as an afterthought. "He would have destroyed a fine example of late nineteenth-century architecture. That building housed a saloon where the town founders might have procured the services of some women of the night."

"It was a brothel?"

"Honey, this was once the Wild West. You couldn't walk fifty yards in any direction without stumbling into a brothel. But if the founders of Mountain Shadow so happened to feel inspired to establish a permanent settlement here while they were enjoying themselves, the building would have *extraordinary* historical significance."

"Uh-huh." The more I talked to Bellamy Broussard, the less I suspected that he'd been the one to poison Jay Mathers. He seemed much too creative and cunning to defeat his enemies with something as unoriginal as murder. "It sounds as though there was no love lost between you and Mathers."

Bellamy rolled his eyes. "Jay Mathers was the sort of man who would have sold out his own grandmother if he thought he could make a quick buck. He was arrogant and underhanded, and — between you and me — the world is better off without him."

"You sound pretty sure of that."

Bellamy's expression darkened. "I never said I wanted him *dead*," he added quickly. "I just said he's better off dead."

"I'm just trying to figure out what happened," I said.

"They arrested my gran in connection with his murder, and —"

"So Mathers really was *murdered*?" Bellamy looked intrigued rather than appalled.

I shrugged. "That's what they're saying."

At those words, Bellamy's eyebrows shot up so high they appeared in danger of disappearing into his faux-windswept hair. "Wait. You don't think *I* had something to do with it? Because I definitely don't have time to stage a murder." He forced an uneasy laugh.

I shook my head. "I don't think you killed him." As desperate as I was to find a likely suspect, I truly didn't believe Bellamy Broussard had had a hand in killing Jay Mathers.

Bellamy shot me an irritated look, as if I'd gotten him worked up for nothing. "Well, if you *insist* on playing detective, you should look into Mathers's business partner, Cliff Estrell. He owns a resort down in Colorado Springs, and the two were on the outs."

Bellamy lowered his voice to a conspiratorial whisper, even though we were the only two people around. "I heard Mathers went behind Estrell's back and tried to purchase some land that he needed for an expansion. If anyone had reason to want Jay Mathers dead, it's him."

CHAPTER THIRTEEN

By some incredible stroke of luck, I'd managed to get the power turned back on at the hotel in time for my meeting with Rusty Coleman — the antique elevator whisperer.

Although Miles the contractor had warned me the old man was hard to get ahold of, Rusty had answered when I'd called and agreed to meet me that afternoon. It meant I'd have to put off going to visit Jay Mathers's business partner, but given Rusty's reputation as a fly-by-night elevator serviceman, I thought it best not to push my luck.

A beat-up red service truck was already parked outside The Grand when Desmond and I drove up. Thinking Des might need to use the bathroom, I opened the passenger-side door, and he hopped out onto the curb like a faithful golden retriever.

I'd expected to find Rusty waiting for me in his truck, but there was no one in the vehicle. Puzzled, I walked up to unlock the front door, only to discover it was already ajar.

I pushed it open a few more inches and heard odd clinking and clanging sounds echoing through the lobby. I knew I hadn't left the door unlocked — not after seeing what vandals had done to the hotel's exterior — and my heart thumped against my ribs.

Desmond must not have thought there was anything amiss, though, because he slinked gracefully around my ankles and pranced into the lobby.

"Hello?" I called, hoping it was Rusty making all that noise and not some vagrant.

No answer.

"Hello?" I took a cautious step inside and followed the noises toward the back of the lobby. My footsteps echoed in the cavernous space, and just on the other side of the staircase, I saw the yellowish glow of a work lamp coming from inside the old Otis elevator. The light gleamed off the intricate scrollwork of the outer cage doors, and I could see a stooped figure moving around inside.

I let out the breath I'd been holding. It *had* to be Rusty. But how had he let himself in?

"Rusty?" I called, poking my head around the corner. The cage door was propped open with a metal weight, and a bearded man dressed in grease-stained overalls was bent over the ancient-looking control panel mounted inside the door. His skin was wrinkled and leathery, his face framed by two of the most wild gray eyebrows I'd ever seen.

He didn't look up at the sound of his name, but his frown seemed to deepen as he shined the light of his headlamp at the dusty collection of wires.

"Rusty?" I repeated, louder this time in case the man was hard of hearing.

"Oh, good. You're here," he grumbled, tilting his head to the side by way of acknowledgement.

"My name is Caroline McCrithers. I'm the new owner of the hotel. Lucille Blackthorne was my aunt."

"I know who you are," Rusty groused. "S'about time somebody called me over to have a look at this lovely lady." He raised his head and gazed up the shaft. "She's been left to rust all these years, poor thing. She needs new cables and new bearings. I can work up a quote."

I pressed my lips together and frowned, chewing awkwardly on the inside of my cheek. I'd heard of people personifying boats and cars, but elevators were a new one for me.

"You plan on allowing guests to ride her?" he asked, still staring up at the system of cables and counterweights as if making some mental calculations.

"Um . . . that was the plan."

Rusty made an aggravated noise in the back of his throat, and I had the feeling that I'd answered incorrectly. "I dunno if she's up to that." He finally lowered his head and fixed me with a penetrating light-blue stare. "All it would take is one group of rowdy kids jumping and making a ruckus — or a guy with a little extra girth . . ." Rusty patted his own flat stomach. "Too much stress, and she could just decide to stop right where she is and stay there 'til the end of time — or until I can come put her right."

I raised my eyebrows. The last thing I needed was guests getting stuck in my elevator "'til the end of time." Then again, there was so much work to be done before I could even *think* about opening the hotel to guests.

"Well, if you don't think you can get the elevator up and running . . ."

"Oh, she'll run just fine," said Rusty emphatically. "Elevators ain't like those battery-powered cars that only got so many good charges in 'em. A fine piece of machinery like Ol' Bertha will outlast us all, so long as she's taken care of."

I assumed Ol' Bertha was the elevator.

Rusty narrowed his eyes and fixed me with an expression one might expect to see from a very strict schoolmarm. "But she won't stand up to dozens of unsupervised little hellions riding up and down at all hours of the day and night."

I couldn't think why I'd ever have "dozens" of unsupervised children running amok at the hotel, but I managed to keep my expression serious as I nodded. "I'll be sure all the little hellions take the stairs."

Rusty frowned at me for such a long time that I wasn't sure my reply had come across as sincere. But then he relented with an indistinct grumble and went back to fussing with the control panel.

"Do I need to loop the electrician in on getting anything rewired?" I asked.

"*Rewired?*" Rusty snapped, wheeling around to glare at me as if I'd uttered something offensive.

I swallowed. "Uh, yeah. You know . . . It was my aunt's last wish that I restore the hotel to its former glory, so I'm trying to make sure everything's up to code."

Rusty let out a huff and braced his hands on his hips. "Now listen here, missy. I've been servicing these beauties for goin' on sixty years. I took care of Ol' Bertha from the time I started 'til The Grand shuttered its doors back in —

oh, seventy-two." He glared at me for effect. "Now, I don't want some county building department yes-man in here messin' with her. Understand?"

I nodded.

"Nobody else touches this elevator besides me."

"Yessir," I muttered, oddly intimidated by this bristle-bearded grease monkey with an undying devotion to my elevator.

There was a long, drawn-out silence. Then Rusty added, almost as an afterthought, "Plus, you don't want to aggravate the spirits."

Up until that point, I'd been willing to absorb just about everything Rusty the elevator whisperer had wanted to throw at me. But at the mention of spirits, there was something like a screeching-brake noise in my mind. "What's that now?"

"Spirits," he barked, as though I were hard of hearing.

"Spirits?" I repeated. "You mean, like, ghosts?"

Rusty gave a jerky nod.

"But there aren't any . . . I mean, you don't *seriously* believe the hotel is haunted?"

"Oh, yeah."

Rusty's tone was lighthearted but firm. Either the man was messing with me, or he believed so ardently in what he was saying that he didn't feel the need to explain.

"The ghost of Roy Wilkerson is probably the most vocal." Rusty jerked his screwdriver toward the upper floors. "He was the hotel handyman way back in the thirties. Legend has it that Ol' Bertha was malfunctioning, and Roy fell down the shaft." Rusty put one greasy index finger to his nose and shook his head. "But I have it on good authority that Roy Wilkerson was pushed."

For a moment, I stared at Rusty, held captive by those eerie blue eyes. "Pushed?"

"Oh, yeah. Roy Wilkerson had been the handyman at this hotel for the better part of thirty years. He wouldn'ta fallen down the elevator shaft."

"Who pushed him?" I asked before I could stop myself.

"Nobody knows. *That's* why he still haunts this place. He's lookin' for his killer." Rusty raised his eyebrows. "They say he was a bad-tempered old codger even in life, and his ghost is not the friendly sort."

I was so taken aback by Rusty's crazy story that I couldn't be bothered to school my expression into something more polite. Rusty gave a creaky-sounding laugh. "Back in the old days, anytime there was a leaky faucet or a toilet overflowed, guests would run screaming from their rooms, claiming to have had a run-in with Roy."

"Roy must be pretty busy these days," I muttered, glancing around at the dilapidated lobby. "There's a lot more than a leaky faucet in need of fixing around here."

This time, Rusty's guffaw came out sounding so much like a bark that Desmond arched his back and hissed.

"Now, don't you go gettin' your nose outta joint, puss," Rusty chided. As he stared down at Desmond, something like recognition gleamed in his eyes, and his whole face lit up. "Say, you look a lot like that snooty old cat that used to follow Miss Lucille around."

"It is her cat," I said. "I inherited Desmond along with this place." I gestured around at the hotel.

"Oh, no. This was probably thirty years ago or more — back when Miss Lucille first bought the place." Rusty chuckled to himself. "I've heard of cats having nine lives, but that would really be somethin'." He cocked his head to the side, examining Desmond, who continued to glare imperiously at him.

I rolled my eyes and gave an involuntary shiver, a little spooked by Rusty's stories and annoyed by the old man's demands. "So don't let kids jump in the elevator and watch out for Roy Wilkerson's ghost. Is that everything?"

"Oh, no." Rusty chuckled. "I could tell you some stories that would curl your hair. Well —" He held out a grease-smeared hand, indicating my frizzy blond rat's nest. "Never mind. But this place is haunted, I can tell ya that. Oh, you'll find all sorts of old hotels that bill themselves as haunted to draw in tourists, but this place is the real deal."

"Hmm," I said, shifting my weight from one foot to the other and wishing I could leave Rusty to his work. It wasn't that I believed in ghosts — I didn't. But something about being all alone in the creaky old hotel with a half-crazy elevator whisperer was giving me the heebee jeebees.

Just then, I heard a muffled clanking noise followed by a dull screech. It sounded like metal rubbing on metal, and I glanced nervously up the elevator shaft. "Is that what it sounds like when it's trying to run?"

"Oh, no. I flipped the breaker so I could work on her box. The old girl just sounds like that sometimes."

I frowned, squinting up at the cables. None appeared to be moving. "You mean . . ."

"I told ya this place was haunted." Rusty chuckled again and returned his attention to the control panel, as if it was totally normal for an elevator to make phantom creaking sounds. "Come here for a second. I wanna show you somethin'."

Something about the casualness with which Rusty proclaimed that my hotel was haunted made me not want to come any closer. But I'd called him out to discuss servicing the ancient Otis, so I shuffled in and peered over his shoulder at the mess of wires inside the panel.

"Back when the hotel changed hands in forty-nine, they closed off the top floor. Nobody has reopened it since, seeing as how it still has the old knob-and-tube wiring. But sometimes this ol' girl acts a little funny, and occasionally she'll take guests up to the fourth floor. It's boarded up, of course — nowhere to go — but it spooks 'em nonetheless."

I squinted at the control panel. "So is there a loose wire or something I need to fix when that happens?"

"Nope!" Rusty reached into his back pocket and produced a grimy business card that showed an illustration of a hand with an eye in the center. "You have any trouble with Bertha droppin' guests on the fourth floor, you just call this gal here, and she'll whip Roy and the rest of 'em into shape."

Numbly, I took the card and stared down at the text. The name was hard to read under the coffee stains and grime, but I could just make out the first name "Jinx" and the title "Medium."

"A *psychic*?" I asked, looking up at Rusty to gauge whether or not he was pulling my leg.

"She ain't just a psychic. I never met a spirit that couldn't be persuaded to settle down with Jinx's help."

For a second, I just stared at him. What kind of repairman suggested a medium for exorcising the spirits from one's antique elevator? I supposed the sort who thought a hotel could indeed be haunted.

"Well, thanks for your help," I said brightly, thinking

I'd need to scour the phonebook for someone who was actually qualified to service antique birdcage elevators.

Rusty seemed oblivious to my dismissal as he screwed the metal faceplate back onto the control panel and patted the cage door fondly. "She's got her quirks, but she runs right as rain. Hang on just a sec. I'll flip the breaker and show ya."

Rusty slipped out of the elevator and disappeared. A moment later, a dim light illuminated the elevator's interior, and I could fully appreciate the stunning detail of the metalwork. Rusty returned to remove the weight holding the door open, and Desmond slinked into the elevator after us, just before the cage door slid closed and the inner door shut along with it.

My chest constricted with an automatic feeling of claustrophobia, and Rusty hit one of the round mother-of-pearl buttons. I staggered backward as the elevator lurched, and then it began to rise with a great creaking and squeaking of cables.

Rusty's smile stretched in a wide grin, and I saw that he was missing several of his front teeth. The elevator stopped on the second floor, and the inner cage door opened automatically.

"Going up." He pushed the button for the third floor, and I was relieved when the elevator stopped rather than clattering up to the boarded-up entrance to the fourth. I wasn't sure if Rusty had been pulling my leg about that, but I wouldn't have put it past the man to prank me by sending us to the now-defunct top story.

When we reached the ground floor again, Rusty pulled the lever that operated the heavy metal door, and I staggered out into the lobby, grateful to be out of Ol' Bertha's gilded cage. Desmond let out a little *ree-arr* and shot out across the parquet floor.

"Well, thank you for agreeing to come out here on such short notice," I said as Rusty began tossing tools back into his dented metal toolbox. "How much do I owe you for the service call?"

"Oh, nothin'," he said, turning his toothless grin on the elevator. "It was a pleasure to have a chance to spend time in the company of such a lovely lady."

I smiled, but somehow I knew he was talking about the elevator and not me.

"I'll work up a bid for the cables and bearings, and you can pay me then."

I nodded and watched Rusty go, unable to ignore the sinking feeling in my gut that Bellamy Broussard had been right. This project wasn't for the faint of heart — nor the inexperienced.

I was just about to follow Rusty out when I heard that odd clanging sound again. It seemed to be coming from one of the upper stories, and now that my superstitious elevator repairman was gone, I felt much more skeptical about any claims of hauntings.

Determined to locate the source of the racket, I climbed back into Ol' Bertha, closed the door, and rode the elevator all the way up to the third floor. The light flickered as I got out, and Desmond came tearing up the steps.

Startled by his sudden appearance, I groped along the wall for a light switch. I flipped it on, and a single fixture down the hallway illuminated the corridor.

In the weak yellowish light, the faded wallpaper, stained pink carpeting, and dusty old fixtures looked much more shabby. I waited to hear the sound again, but the horrid clanging had stopped.

I let out a huff. Perhaps owning an old hotel was going to be like having a car that made a funny noise. Every time you took it into the shop to investigate, it suddenly wouldn't make that sound.

I was just about to go back downstairs when a loud creak made me jump. It sounded as though someone were walking on the floor above me, but that was impossible. Wasn't it?

I shivered. Maybe Rusty had forgotten something and had sneaked upstairs when I wasn't looking. But he couldn't have made it all the way to the fourth floor, could he?

Pushing open the nearest door, I crossed the room and peered out the window to the deserted street below. Rusty's truck was gone.

Thinking I must be hearing things, I backed out of the room and shut the door. But then I heard another groan of the floorboards, and Desmond tilted his head to look at the ceiling.

"You heard it, too?" I asked, my voice low with dread.

For a moment, I considered calling the police. I didn't truly believe the hotel was haunted, and it made me uneasy to think I might have some very real vagrants squatting up there.

But then Rusty's ghost stories slid to the forefront of my mind. Surely rumors of the haunted hotel were part of local lore. Officer Hamby would think I was a ninny if I called him out to investigate and there turned out to be nothing there.

No. I needed to put on my big-girl pants and investigate on my own. If someone *was* up there, I could call the police then.

Desmond led the way down the hallway toward the door at the very end. Reaching into my purse, I dug out the long brass skeleton key I'd found among Lucille's possessions after my meeting with the contractor. The end was shaped like a three-leaf clover and bore the same engraved leather fob as the key R.P. had given me. I suspected it had been the hotel master key back when The Grand had first opened.

I fitted the old key into the lock and felt the bolt draw back as I turned it. The door opened with a loud creak, and Desmond slinked between my legs and up the dark, dusty staircase.

CHAPTER FOURTEEN

The deafening creaks and moans of the floorboards were the only sounds I heard as I climbed the stairs to the fourth floor. Luckily, I'd remembered to bring one of Gran's flashlights with me this time, so I could see where I was going as I reached the landing.

The faces in the portraits that lined the walls loomed through the dark, and once again I got the unsettling feeling that their eyes were following me down the hall. The ghosts of furniture covered in sheets greeted me as I shined my flashlight into the first room. Swirls of dust gleamed in the narrow beam of light, but I didn't hear or see anything.

Room by room, I searched the floor for any sign that someone had been camping out in the hotel. But apart from some shards of glass and crushed beer cans littering the corner of one room, it didn't look as though anyone besides me and Miles had been up there in ages.

It had begun to rain outside again, and the sound of raindrops hitting the windowpanes added to the haunted feel of the place. My spine tingled as I pushed open the door at the very end of the hall, and Desmond gave an excited yowl. He scampered into the room and bounded across the bed, his yellow eyes flashing in the dark.

I didn't know why, but something about this room made me uneasy. Goosebumps pricked all along my arms, and I felt an uncomfortable tingle on the back of my neck. The rain was coming down harder by then, and I could hear the tinny patter of drops hitting the vents on the roof.

Shuffling slowly toward the bathroom, I caught a glimpse of my reflection in the cracked mirror over the dresser, and my heart leapt to my throat.

"It's only you," I whispered, staring at my pale reflection and trying to slow my breathing. "There's no one else here."

"Yes, dear. Just the three of us."

The voice seemed to cut right through the dark, and this time my heart gave an alarming jolt. I wheeled around to look behind me, but there was no one else there.

"Hello?" I called, hardly able to hear my own voice over the pounding in my ears.

No answer.

I kept turning in a slow circle, locking eyes with my reflection again. Desmond blinked at me from the bed, and the sound of his rumbling purrs filled the room.

"What the . . ."

This time I was *certain* I hadn't imagined anything. The voice had been too distinct to have been a trick of the wind howling outside or some other old-building noise.

Still breathing hard and fast, I poked my head into the bathroom, which for some reason creeped me out way more than the main suite. The scent of mildew wafted up to greet me, but there was no serial killer lurking in the shadows — just an old clawfoot tub, a cracked toilet, a sink, and a puddle of water.

I looked up and saw a bulge in the ceiling where water from a leak had collected. Dead leaves were matted in the space between the toilet and vanity, as if some animal had been nesting there.

"I am losing my mind," I muttered, turning back toward the bed.

"I hope not, darling. You're the best hope we've got."

I jerked my head up at the sound of the voice and came face to face with Aunt Lucille.

I wasn't immediately sure how I knew it was her, seeing as how the woman before me couldn't have been a day over thirty. She was sprawled across the brocade settee, dressed in a strapless satin number that was short enough to reveal long, toned legs in fishnet stockings.

I took an automatic step back, chest heaving and heart thundering. This wasn't my ninety-eight-year-old great-aunt. It was the playbill version of Lucille. She was even in black and white!

"Aunt Lucille," I whispered, blinking several times in the hope that the hallucination would subside.

"Oh, *good*. You can finally see me. I was worried you might not have gotten enough of the Blackthorne gene for me to actually make a connection."

"The Blackthorne gene?" I repeated, inching back until I felt my butt hit the wall.

Hearing voices was bad enough, but *seeing* things? I needed to lie down.

"Oh, don't look so alarmed. All the women in our line have it — other than Virginia. She was always so *literal*."

Lucille tucked her knees together, swung her legs around, and got to her feet.

As she did, I realized that I could see right *through* her, almost as if she were a projection or . . . No, I wasn't going to go there.

"Oh, I'm so sorry. I didn't mean to scare you, darling."

I shook my head, sank down onto the dusty carpet, and rested my back against the wall. I must have still been hung over, or maybe I hadn't eaten enough for lunch. I *had* skipped breakfast that morning and gone straight to the arraignment. That was the only explanation for why I was seeing the ghost of my aunt Lucille!

"You're not real," I breathed, closing my eyes and leaning my head against the wall.

"Of course I'm not *real*," Lucille balked. "I did *die*, you know."

"Why is this happening?" I groaned to myself, pressing my fingertips into my eyelids and willing Lucille to disappear. "I'm doing your bidding. You don't need to haunt me!"

"*Haunt* you?" Aunt Lucille sounded hurt and offended. "Is that what you think I'm doing? Well, I won't bother helping if you'd rather handle it on your own, though I've been told I have an eye for decorating. Plus, it will give us a chance to spend some time together."

For a hallucination, Lucille sure had a lot of personality. And even though I knew it was all coming from my own subconscious, I couldn't help but open my eyes to take in the stunning figment of my imagination.

Lucille looked just as I'd always imagined the beautiful free-spirited burlesque dancer who'd parlayed her singing and dancing skills into a career as an actress. Long black curls were heaped atop her head, and she wore dark, dramatic lipstick. Her eyebrows had been stenciled thick and full, giving her a playful, flirtatious look. Her neck and wrists were dripping with what I could only assume were fake diamonds, but she was in her bare stocking feet as if she'd come up to the room to lounge.

"Why are you here?" I asked after a moment, thinking that if I could tease out whatever stressor had triggered the hallucination, I might be able to get rid of it.

"I'm not sure," she mused, propping one glittering hand on her hip and looking around as if she'd forgotten. "One minute I was dead — caught in between this world and the next. And then . . ." She gave an exaggerated shrug. "Well, I don't remember what happened after that, but at least I get to spend my days in my beloved hotel. Although, I'll be the first to admit that it could use some work . . ." She frowned up at the cracked ceiling and the light fixture coated in a quarter inch of dust. Then she looked back to me, and I caught a flicker of inspiration in her eyes. "Maybe I was sent back to help *you*."

I groaned. I didn't want to offend Lucille — even if she was a figment of my imagination — but the last thing I needed on top of everything else was to be seeing ghosts.

"Caroline." Her chastising tone drew my attention. She sounded just like Gran. "What's happened?"

I let out a slow breath through my mouth. Talking to oneself was the first sign of insanity, but maybe speaking my problems out loud would help me process whatever trauma had led to my mind breaking.

"Well, let's see . . . my fiancé turned out to be a fraud . . . I've inherited this massive haunted hotel that I have *no* idea what to do with . . . Gran is the number-one suspect in a murder investigation, and I have to stay here until she goes to trial — or until I can figure out who the real killer is."

Lucille's heavily penciled eyebrows shot up. "*Murder*? What do you mean, murder?"

"I mean this developer guy was killed, and Gran was the last person to see him alive. And the cookies she brought him tested positive for poison."

Lucille shook her head slowly, eyebrows creeping even higher. "Well, I'm not sure what to do about that. Are you sure she didn't kill him?"

For a moment, I just gaped at my hallucination.

"Oh, don't look at me like that. I was only teasing. I'm sure it will all work out. As for the lying fiancé, I've had my share of those, darling. Trust me when I say that men cannot be relied upon to bring you lasting happiness. Only diamonds are forever."

I let out a long sigh and closed my eyes again. For a hallucination, Lucille was pretty insightful. Maybe I was saner and wiser than I gave myself credit for.

"What's the problem with the hotel?" she probed.

"The *problem*?" I opened my eyes and waved my hands around at the musty carpet and cracked plaster walls. "The problem is that this place is a contractor's dream. The roof leaks, the electrical isn't up to code, the floor is rotting, all the rooms need to be gutted . . . oh, and apparently the elevator is haunted."

"The whole hotel is haunted!" Lucille exclaimed, throwing up her hands with a laugh as if I were bringing up a bunch of non-problems. "Roy *is* rather a grouch, but he's an old softie once you get to know him. And I've found many of the other resident spirits quite pleasant and welcoming."

I decided not to dig in on my assertion that there was no such thing as ghosts. It seemed a moot point when I was arguing with . . . a ghost. "Aunt Lucille, when you're trying to reopen an upscale hotel, 'resident spirits' are a bug, not a feature."

"I'm sure I don't know what you mean. I only had one brush with bed bugs in all the times I stayed here, and the manager was *most* apologetic."

I shook my head. Apparently my subconscious was sharp enough to realize that the *real* Aunt Lucille wouldn't have understood the expression.

Well played, Caroline's subconscious. Well played.

"Listen, Aunt Lucille. As much as I would like to give up being a marketing goon and fulfill your dying wish to revive a charming historic hotel, I really don't think I'm gonna be able to find a way to swing that."

"Oh, darling. Money is easy. You can *always* find the money. Look at me." She lifted her head and stretched out her arms like an actress inviting applause. "I grew up a poor farm girl in Kansas. We never had two pennies to rub together. I got a job sweeping up at the barber shop in our little town, saved up everything I could, and hopped a train out west. I got hired on as a maid here at The Grand, and one evening, the night's entertainment had laryngitis. The manager told me to put on her dress and sing to keep the guests drinking and dancing . . . The rest is history. I've performed on the largest stages in North America. I've stayed in the most luxurious five-star hotels. I've been wined and dined by millionaires, politicians, and titans of industry . . . I ate oysters Rockefeller with John F. Kennedy!"

"I hate to break it to you, Aunt Lucille, but you died poor."

"Is that what R.P. told you?" Lucille threw up her hands. "This is why lawyers and accountants are never any fun. They're afraid to enjoy their money." She gestured around. "This hotel brought me joy in life, and it still brings me joy in death. And I know for a *fact* that it's worth at least half a million dollars, or else that vulture Jay Mathers wouldn't have been sniffing around."

At the mention of Mathers, that now-familiar tightness returned to my chest. My mind started to race, and I had to expend great effort to draw a full breath.

Gran was in trouble. R.P. had said as much. I couldn't afford to lose my mind. Gran's life depended on me keeping it together. I had to find Jay Mathers's true killer, and I couldn't do that if I was busy talking to a hallucination.

"I don't have time for this," I said, mostly to myself. "I have to go."

I don't know why I added that last bit. Aunt Lucille was just a figment of my imagination. There was no need to be polite.

I heard an irritated yowl and looked back over my shoulder for Desmond, only to find him twining himself between the legs of his former mistress.

"This discussion isn't over, young lady!"

"Yes, it is!" I called, half running from the room.

I was finished with ghosts. First thing tomorrow, I was going to raid the yellow pages to find a *qualified* elevator repairman — and possibly a psychiatrist — but right then I had to get out of that infernal hotel.

As soon as Des followed me into the stairwell, I slammed the door shut behind me. For a moment I feared the hallucinations wouldn't stop, but Aunt Lucille's ghost didn't follow.

CHAPTER FIFTEEN

Rain was coming down in icy sheets by the time I locked the door of the hotel behind me. Desmond flattened his ears to his head, and when I started running for the car, he stayed right where he was and glared at me from beneath the tattered overhang.

Growling under my breath, I doubled back to grab him,tucking him into the folds of my jacket and dashing through the rain. The Pinto's leather seats were cold as I folded myself into the car. I cranked the heat, but I couldn't stop shaking. I needed to clear my head.

The neon-purple sign for Déjà Brew beamed through the haze as I drove through downtown. I parked on the street and sprinted for the entrance, leaving Desmond to glare out at the offending storm and lick his disheveled fur.

"Back so soon?" came Amber's chipper voice as I rushed into the warmth of the café. She glanced up from behind the espresso machine, and her expression instantly changed. "Whoa. Are you okay?"

"Yeah. Why?" My voice came out as a high-pitched squeak, and I hurriedly swiped under my eyes for any offending makeup smears. I was sure my hair was a frizzy mess, but I didn't want Amber to think I was a train wreck all the time.

"You look as though you've seen a ghost." She chuckled to herself and started pouring the milk for my mocha.

When I didn't respond right away, she glanced up, and her easy smile faded.

"Would you think I was crazy if I told you I had?" I kept my tone light so I could brush it off as a joke, but I held Amber's gaze.

To my surprise, she just laughed. "Pssh. Nope. That's just Mountain Shadow."

I stared.

"Why?" Amber pounded the portafilter on the edge of the drip tray as though we were talking about the weather. "Did you see the ghost of that guy who was murdered back in the thirties?"

"No," I said, collapsing in the chair nearest the counter and shivering despite the warmth of the café. "Though if it had been him, maybe he could have told me who killed him."

"Right?" Amber chuckled. I was pretty sure she thought I was joking.

I fell silent watching her make my drink, comforted by the rich scent of espresso and the familiar clangs and clunks of Amber fiddling with the machine.

"I'm surprised the police haven't been in to question me yet," she added, almost as an afterthought.

"Why?" I asked, suddenly alert.

"That developer guy's assistant was in here every morning picking up his coffee order — ten 'til seven on the dot."

I sat up straighter in my seat, my mind buzzing with this new information. "D-did she come in the morning he was killed?"

Amber frowned, trying to remember. "I think so. I'd have to look at my receipts. She always paid with her company card, so it wouldn't be hard to find out."

"Could you look now?" I asked, very aware of how desperate I sounded.

Amber looked up at me, clearly bewildered by the urgency in my voice.

"They arrested my gran for Jay Mathers's murder," I confessed. "Obviously she didn't kill him. I've been trying to figure out who did."

"Oh." Amber's eyes widened, and in that moment, under all her piercings and tattoos, she looked incredibly young. "Y-yeah. I'll check."

She finished pouring my mocha and went over to the little tablet mounted to the counter that she used to take customer orders. I followed her over to the register and watched with bated breath as she scrolled through the morning's transactions.

"Yep," she said after a moment, her eyes flashing with excitement. "Right here." She turned the tablet toward me to show an order for an extra-large flat white. "I rang her up at six fifty-two."

My heart hammered in my throat.

"Is there any way you could print me out a copy of that transaction?"

"Sure." Amber fiddled with the tablet some more, and I

heard the high-pitched rip of the machine printing out a receipt. She handed it over, and I stared at the date and time printed in purple ink. Sure enough, Monica had bought an extra-large flat white early Friday morning.

I let out a long breath, turning the assistant's story over in my head. R.P. had said Mathers hadn't had anything in his stomach other than the cookies. Monica couldn't have poisoned his coffee. So why had she lied about seeing him the morning he was killed?

It was possible she was just scared and didn't want the police looking at her as a suspect, but my gut told me there was more to the story. I tucked the receipt into my Filofax, thanked Amber, and ducked back out into the driving rain.

I didn't know how Monica fit into all this, but I was determined to find out.

I awoke the next morning after a restless night's sleep, determined to pay Monica a visit. But when I drove up to the Mathers Properties building, I found the office door locked and the windows dark. I didn't know where Monica lived, so I decided to switch gears and visit Cliff Estrell — Jay Mathers's former business partner.

Estrell owned The Aspenwood in Colorado Springs — a sprawling luxury resort and world-renowned golf course nestled at the foot of Cheyenne Mountain. The crown jewel of the AAA five-diamond resort was the eight-hundred-room hotel, surrounded by immaculately groomed gardens, glittering pools, tennis courts, a luxury spa, and a host of fine-dining options.

During high season, the weekend rate for a single room was about seven hundred bucks. And if you wanted a room with a view, that would set you back an extra two hundred. Adding to the air of exclusivity was the six-foot-high stone wall that surrounded the property, along with the four huge wrought-iron gates blocking every entrance.

Fortunately, I'd done my homework. While drooling over photos of the fancy European-inspired decor and plush-looking beds, I'd learned that it was possible to gain access to The Aspenwood without being a guest if one was there to golf. I'd also stumbled across a *Business Insider* article from twenty seventeen that said Cliff Estrell started his day with nine holes of golf at his exclusive resort.

The green fee at The Aspenwood was a steep three hundred bucks, but I'd dusted off one of my credit cards in the hope that I'd be able to gain access to Cliff Estrell and question him about his relationship with Mathers. The man working the gate looked skeptical when I told him I was there to golf, but I'd found Gramps's old clubs in the garage and propped them up in the front seat for realism.

I was still cringing over the outrageous green fee as I pulled through the gate and found a parking spot. Besides the occasional clap of a golf club and the distant *thwop* of a ball hitting the ground, the fairway was quiet that morning. The scent of freshly mowed grass and fertilizer wafted up to greet me as I wrestled my dusty clubs out of the car.

As soon as I'd heaved the heavy bag onto my shoulder, I realized I might have been overly optimistic to think I'd be able to casually bump into Cliff Estrell. The golf course was absolutely enormous, and the other players were just khaki- and neon-clad specks on the gleaming green horizon.

But then an angry voice caught my attention, and I turned in the direction of the noise. An older man dressed in khaki shorts and a tangerine golf shirt was arguing with the young Hispanic golf-cart attendant. The golfer's silver-gray hair gleamed in the early-morning sun, and his back was soaked with sweat.

"That cart you gave me left me stranded on the fifth hole!" he groused at the attendant. "I've told Roger a hundred times to get the duds out of the fleet and send them off for maintenance!"

"I'm so sorry, Mr. Estrell. I'll get you another cart right away."

Mr. Estrell. The man shouting at the golf-cart attendant was *the* Cliff Estrell. In that moment, I honestly couldn't believe my luck.

Estrell continued to grumble as the attendant raced around getting him another set of keys. "Get rid of that cart. I want it off the fairway! This is a premier resort favored by the best pros in the country. What is the *matter* with you?"

"I'm so sorry, sir. Mr. Halliday recently replaced the battery in that one, and I ran all of them myself this morning."

A dangerous look flashed through the old man's eyes as he glared at the attendant. "Are you calling me a liar?"

"N-no, sir."

"It's not the battery, you idiot. It's probably a faulty solenoid. Roger would know that if he'd worked on the cart for more than five minutes!"

"I'll let Mr. Halliday know right away."

As the attendant ran off to pull Estrell's golf cart

around, I drew in a breath and approached the building. "Mr. Estrell?"

The old man whirled around, and I tried very hard to smile despite the feeling that I was about to be yelled at. I'd thought through what I would say to Estrell and practiced it on the way over, but as those wolflike eyes locked on to mine, any thought of how I would broach the topic evaporated from my mind.

"*Yes?*" he prompted with an edge of impatience.

"I-I'm Caroline McCrithers," I choked, my shoulders crumpling under his stare.

"I don't know a Caroline McCrithers," he said, turning away with a dismissive eye roll as though I were the paparazzi or something.

"I-I know," I said quickly, unable to come up with anything in that moment other than the truth. "I was there the day . . . the day Jay Mathers died."

That caught his attention. Estrell swiveled back around to face me, and I fought the urge to shrink away from his predatory stare.

"My grandmother is being held in connection with Mr. Mathers's death," I said in a breathless voice. "I-I've been trying to piece together what happened to him and clear my grandmother's name."

"What *happened* to him?" Estrell hissed, his eyes narrowing to slits. "Jay Mathers got about as much as he deserved. The world is better off without him."

I opened my mouth, but no words came out. I wasn't sure what I'd been expecting Estrell to say, but it certainly wasn't that. "That may be true, sir, but I can't let my ninety-two-year-old grandmother spend the rest of her life in prison for a crime she didn't commit."

"Well, I'm sorry," said Estrell, not sounding sorry at all as the attendant pulled up in a brand-new golf cart. "But I'm afraid I can't help you."

He was just about to climb into the cart and speed off to finish his round of golf when an unexpected surge of anger flared in my gut. Here was a man who thought he was above everyone and everything. Gran was about to stand trial for murder. I'd paid three hundred bucks to gain access to Estrell's stupid resort in the hope of running into him, and he couldn't even take two minutes to give me the information I'd come for.

Before I had a moment to consider my actions, I followed Estrell to the golf cart and positioned myself directly in front of it. "You and Mathers used to be partners," I said quietly. "I think you know why he was killed, and I'm not leaving until I learn the reason."

Estrell rolled his eyes and turned to the attendant, as if considering having him call security. But just then a group of men and their caddies pulled up in front of the building, and I knew instinctively that Estrell wouldn't have me dragged out of there when there were wealthy guests watching.

"I heard you and Mathers had a deal that went bad," I continued, blazing on despite the tight feeling in my chest.

"I didn't *kill* him," Estrell growled softly, his anger competing with his desire not to be overheard.

"But you know who else might want him dead."

Estrell dragged in a long breath, his nostrils flaring as he considered what to tell me. "Mathers had a lot of irons in the fire. Inevitably, some of those deals went bad — either because they were bad to begin with, or because

Mathers ran out of money and reneged on his commitments. I'm sure there is no shortage of people who would be happy to see him six feet under."

"I need specifics."

"Well, I can't give you those." Estrell jerked his head around to look at me. "Jay was very tight-lipped about the deals he was working. He was extremely superstitious that way."

"But you must know someone —"

Estrell opened his mouth to cut me off, but at that moment, a man in a khaki hat and uniform shirt came ambling over, and Estrell turned his attention to him. "Roger. Finally."

As Estrell's wolfish eyes snapped on to him, the man's already ashen face seemed to drain of all color. The change that came over Estrell was equally dramatic. Gone was the cagey old man afraid of causing a scene. The arrogant, ruthless resort owner was back in an instant, brushing me off with a curt, "Excuse me."

I blinked at the abrupt dismissal, watching Estrell explain the golf-cart situation to the man called Roger, who appeared to be in charge of the green. I'd expected Estrell to pull the man off to the side, but instead he began berating him loudly for allowing the cart to remain in the fleet.

Stumbling toward the pro shop, a mixture of horror and pity came over me as I set my bag on the ground and pretended to fiddle with my clubs. The sound of Estrell's dressing-down echoed over the pavement, and the men who'd just finished their game hurried inside the clubhouse to avoid the spectacle.

Apparently, everyone there knew Cliff Estrell, and no one was surprised by his outburst. The thought that stuck with me as I walked back to my car was that if a faulty golf cart could cause such offense, there was almost nothing Estrell wouldn't do to get even with a man who had wronged him.

CHAPTER SIXTEEN

Jay Mathers's wife Claudia was next on my list of potential suspects, though it took most of Wednesday morning just to track her down. When I'd called the house, her assistant had told me Mrs. Mathers was at the spa, trying to soothe her nerves after the shock of her husband's death.

I wasn't sure *which* spa, so after my little chat with Estrell, I sat in the car and called every spa and health club in the area to tell them I had an urgent message for Claudia. I'd just about given up when I found her at The Lotus Leaf just a few miles from The Aspenwood. I booked myself a foot treatment over the phone — the cheapest service available — and arrived forty-five minutes before my scheduled appointment.

The Lotus Leaf was clearly one of the more high-end establishments, and everything from the stonework counter in the reception area to the inset fountain in the entryway oozed luxury and comfort. Relaxing flute music was playing softly over the sound system, and a subtle but expensive-smelling mint-eucalyptus fragrance pervaded every corner.

A demur woman dressed all in black informed me that the facilities were available for me to use before and after my treatment, so I went into the locker room to don my soft white robe before heading to the poolside lounge.

On the patio overlooking the pool, waiters in dapper black waistcoats floated between tables, bringing wealthy-looking middle-aged women glasses of cucumber water, bright kale salads, and platters of gorgeously plated wasabi salmon garnished with sunflower sprouts.

Taking a seat near the edge of the lounge, I surreptitiously scanned the crowd for any sign of Claudia Mathers. I'd found her photo in an online article about the couple's philanthropic efforts, and I was confident I'd be able to spot her.

Claudia wasn't dining on the patio, nor was she lounging by the pool or soaking in the hot tub. By the time I wandered inside for my Splendor Complete Foot Therapy — also known as a fancy foot rub — I was beginning to lose heart. Either Mrs. Mathers had retreated to her room for the day, or she was being pampered into oblivion with back-to-back treatments.

Thinking I might as well try to unwind for a few minutes before driving back up the pass, I traded my heavy terrycloth robe for a skimpy white towel and headed into the sauna.

As I stepped through the door into the heat, the same enticing mint-eucalyptus scent wafted out to greet me. The sauna was a small, tastefully appointed room lit with discreet can lighting. Polished cedar benches snaked along the walls, and rolled white towels were stacked neatly by the door. There was only one other guest inside, and I was so shocked to see her there that I almost dropped my towel.

Claudia Mathers was reclined on the far bench with two little purple things stuck under her eyes. She wore a towel and a pair of spa sandals, and her fluffy auburn hair was pulled back with a headband. She didn't lift her head when I walked in, and I figured she was too blissed-out to notice me.

I settled on the bench adjacent to Claudia and gave a theatrical, satisfied sigh. "So nice," I murmured, leaning back against the bench as the hot, dry air pressed in around me.

Claudia didn't reply, and it took me a moment to think of something else to say. Spa etiquette dictated that I should keep my mouth shut, but I wasn't about to leave without learning whether Claudia was a viable suspect.

"What treatment is that?" I asked, deciding to jump right in and hope that she was open to having a conversation.

Claudia grudgingly lifted one wrinkled eyelid. "It's a green-tea rejuvenating eye mask."

"Ah," I said, nervously bunching and unbunching the hem of my towel. "I had the most *amazing* foot treatment before this — like a hundred little angels massaging my arches." I wiggled my feet for emphasis.

"Sounds lovely," Claudia muttered, plainly irritated that I was still talking.

I glanced down at her toes, which, unlike mine, were freshly polished. As I searched for an icebreaker other than "Hey, I heard you killed your husband," my gaze landed on the thin silver anklet with a turquoise Kokopelli charm.

"I like your anklet," I said, trying for friendly rather than annoying.

Claudia's eyebrows lifted, and her expression softened. "Thank you," she said with all sincerity, straightening up as she turned to look at me. "My late husband *hated* it."

Jackpot.

"O-oh," I stammered, taken aback. I honestly hadn't expected such an easy opening, but I kept my expression carefully blank and remembered my manners in the nick of time. "I'm sorry. Did you, *er*, lose him recently?"

"Very recently," said Claudia, lifting her eyebrows.

I swallowed to wet my dry throat. I was already perspiring because of the sauna, but I could now smell the nervous sweat I sometimes got before a big presentation. "H-how did he die?"

Claudia drew a deep breath and leaned closer, suddenly delighted to have someone to talk to. "He was murdered."

"Oh, no!" I said, clapping a hand to my mouth. I hoped that was the appropriate response. Claudia had said it so matter-of-factly that I wasn't actually sure how I was supposed to react. "I'm *so* sorry."

Claudia waved my apology away.

"Do, uh . . . Do the police know who did it?"

She shook her head. "I heard they made an arrest, but I'd be surprised if they managed to get it right the first time." She glanced up to meet my eyes. "No need to look so sad on my account. It was *not* a love match. Well, perhaps it was once, but the bloom has been off the rose for quite some time."

"Oh?" I tried not to appear too eager.

She nodded and lowered her voice. "My husband has always had, shall we say, a *wandering eye*."

I opened my mouth and then closed it again. I was at a loss for words, but I needed to know more. If Jay Mathers had been having an affair, that was certainly motive for murder. "How can you be sure?"

Claudia's gaze flickered down to my bare ring finger, which I curled self-consciously into my palm. I'd taken Todd's ring to a pawn shop to confirm it was a fake before tossing it dramatically into Lake Michigan.

"You're not married."

I shook my head.

Claudia nodded sagely. "When you've been with the same man for as long as I have, you just know. Oh, they usually make an effort to hide it at first, but there are always signs."

"Like what?" I croaked, embarrassed by how badly I wanted this information.

Claudia wrinkled her nose. "You'll catch them lying about silly little things, like where they ate lunch or whom they were with on such-and-such night. Suddenly, they're dressing nicer or wearing different cologne. Then they're working late on a big project, or they're always on their phone."

My chest tightened. Claudia's signs of cheating sounded a lot like Todd's behavior, minus the nice clothes and cologne. This confirmed my theory that he'd been two-timing me on top of everything else, and I got a fresh pang of nausea in my gut.

My disgust and misery must have shown on my face, because Claudia reached over and patted my knee.

"The first time I accused him, he was so angry. The

second time, it was much less dramatic. He acted as though it were *my* fault, the cad. After that . . ." She trailed off sadly. "One day, I woke up and realized that the man I'd married was never going to be faithful. I just *knew* he was seeing that little sprig of a thing who worked for him. I'd take off for a week at a time and come home to find another woman's lipstick on the sheets or a long blond hair in the shower drain."

My mind instantly went to Monica, the assistant. If she'd been having an affair with her boss, it would explain why she'd lied about seeing him that morning. If the police had learned about the affair, she'd be a prime suspect. It also explained why she'd been so quick to leap to Mathers's defense — and why she'd seemed so upset about his death.

Claudia's face had taken on a far-off look, and the knot in my chest tightened. "Why did you stay with him?" I asked quietly.

"I may have been naïve going into the marriage, but I'm no fool!" She let out a sharp breath through her nose. "Jay was a lot of things, but he wasn't poor. I haven't worked a day in my life, and as payment for twenty-two miserable years of marriage, I won't have to start now."

I chewed on my bottom lip, dying to ask the question that was burning on my tongue. "Given the affairs and your relationship with your husband . . . aren't *you* a suspect?"

Claudia certainly had a motive — especially if Jay had wanted a divorce.

"Because it's always the wife?" Mrs. Mathers gave a soft chuckle. "No. Fortunately, I was out of the country at the time of Jay's death. I only learned of his passing after my return."

"That must have been quite a shock."

"Not really, no."

I wasn't sure what my face was doing, but Mrs. Mathers saw fit to clarify. "One shouldn't speak ill of the dead, but Jay did not win many friends in his line of work. He was *ruthless* when it came to business."

"How so?"

Claudia sucked in a heaving breath. "Jay was a real-estate developer. He didn't care what he had to destroy to put a dollar in his pocket. I don't think there was *anyone* he wouldn't have double-crossed if he thought he could profit from the deal. Take his business partner. He bought a prominent resort about ten years ago, and for a while, he and Jay were working together on the expansion. Jay offered to fund the construction of the new facilities if his partner secured the land. His partner could keep his capital freed up to continue to renovate the resort, and Jay would receive a share of the profits.

"Well, Jay discovered a home just south of the golf course that belonged to one of the workers at the resort. It had been in his family for generations, but the worker had fallen into ill health and gotten behind on his property taxes, so Jay bought the tax lien. He wanted to secure the title to the property so he could turn around and sell it to his partner at an outrageously inflated price. Of course, his partner learned of the scheme and made the worker an offer, but the damage was already done."

I sucked in a deep breath. Jay Mathers had been even more heartless than I'd thought. He'd taken advantage of a sick man with the intent of screwing over his business partner. Not only did it add credence to my theory that Cliff Estrell may have killed Jay Mathers, but it added another suspect to my list.

"I don't know who killed him," Claudia sighed. "Only that they did me a favor."

CHAPTER SEVENTEEN

The scent of scorched butter and burnt sugar wafted up to greet me as I walked through Gran's front door. The air was thick and heavy with smoke, and I could hear Gran cursing softly as she clattered around in the kitchen.

"Mother Theresa!" she groused, pulling a tray of what looked like lumps of coal out of the smoking oven.

I wrinkled my nose and hurried over to help, grabbing a dish towel to use as a potholder and ferrying the burnt cookies out to the back porch to avoid stinking up the house any further.

"What happened?" I called as I came back inside, taking in the scene of disarray.

Gran had hauled out her electric mixer and what looked like every cookie sheet she owned. The counter was covered in flour, torn butter wrappers, eggshells, and an upturned bottle of vanilla extract.

"What does it look like?" Gran shot back. "I left the cookies in the oven and forgot to set a timer."

"Uh-huh." I took in the sight of Gran's royal-blue tracksuit dusted with flour and the painful-looking burn on her hand.

In all the times I'd visited her, she'd probably made me her ginger cookies at least four or five dozen times. I'd never once known her to forget to set a timer — or burn anything, for that matter.

"I'm going to figure out who really killed Jay Mathers," I told her. "You're not going to jail."

"Well, aren't you the queen of non sequiturs?"

I cocked my head to the side and gave her a pointed look. Gran puckered her lips in irritation. "Oh, all *right*. So I'm a little out of sorts. I did spend a night in *jail*, you know. I was propositioned by no fewer than two surly young ladies, and my own granddaughter didn't have the decency to bake me a cake with a file in it!"

"I'm pretty sure the cops have caught on to the ol' nail-file-in-a-cake trick, Gran," I said, grabbing the garbage can from under the sink and sweeping the eggshells and butter wrappers into it. "Even in Mountain Shadow."

Gran lifted her chin. "It still would have been nice if you'd tried."

"I'm trying to figure out who really killed Jay Mathers so we can clear your name."

"*You're* going to clear my name?" Gran sounded doubtful.

"I'm going to try." I collapsed into one of the ladder-back chairs crowded around her kitchen table and pulled out my Filofax to take down some notes. "I just had a very interesting conversation with Mathers's wife."

"If *Forensic Files* has taught me anything, it's that it's usually the spouse," said Gran.

"That's what I thought, but Claudia claims she was out of the country when her husband was killed. I suppose she could have had someone working for her, but it doesn't explain how your cookies tested positive for strychnine. She would have had to bribe someone at the lab to tamper with the results, which I'm not even sure is possible. And how would she know you were going to bring Mathers cookies in the first place?"

"It doesn't make sense," Gran agreed. "I'll be darned if I know how strychnine ended up in my cookies."

That piece was the part that bothered me the most — the idea that someone had set Gran up.

"You still haven't told me the real reason you went to see him." I didn't believe for one second that Gran had gone there to gloat.

"I don't want to talk about it," she grumbled.

"We're going to have to talk about it sometime."

"Well, not today."

Seeing that I wasn't going to get anywhere with that line of questioning, I shut my mouth and looked down at my planner. On one page, I had my scant notes about Mathers's murder, and right beside it was the number of the funeral director.

"Well, if you don't want to talk about what you were doing at Mathers's office, we should talk about Lucille's memorial," I said. "Were you thinking open casket, closed casket, or cremation?"

For a moment, Gran looked thoughtful. Then a spark of mischief lit her eyes. "There's a really nice reservoir about forty minutes from here. Why don't we float the old girl out to sea, shoot off some fireworks, and light 'er up?"

"I'm pretty sure a Viking funeral is out of the question,

but cremation should be no problem." I made a note in my planner, deciding that if Gran wasn't going to take this seriously, I'd make the arrangements on my own. "I'll call the funeral director tomorrow. How's Monday for the service?"

"Fine," said Gran, waving a dismissive hand.

"She was your *sister*, you know," I said, my irritation getting the better of me. "The least you could do is help me give Lucille a nice memorial service."

"Lucille and I had hardly spoken in the last thirty years," Gran snapped.

"And whose fault was that?" I shot back, unable to keep my thoughts to myself.

I might have imagined seeing Lucille's ghost at the hotel, but the hallucination had reminded me of what a vibrant, loving person she'd been. I couldn't understand what she could have done to make her sister angry enough to disown her.

"*Hers*," said Gran stubbornly. "Though Lucille always loved to play the victim."

"I don't understand. What did she do that was so bad?"

"I don't want to talk about it, Caroline. I'm tired."

"Fine," I said, throwing up my hands and pulling my laptop toward me. If Gran and Lucille hadn't buried the hatchet in thirty years, I didn't think there was anything I could say that would put her in a forgiving mood. So I opened my computer and did a quick search for "strychnine poisoning" to try to solve our more immediate problem of Gran's murder charges.

I pulled up an article from the CDC and read the first few paragraphs. "It says here that strychnine poisoning can result from drinking contaminated water, eating contaminated food, inhaling the substance, or even absorbing it through the skin. Symptoms of poisoning usually appear within fifteen to sixty minutes, so Mathers probably ingested it between seven fifteen and eight o'clock." I turned to Gran. "I don't suppose you have an alibi you'd like to share with the class?"

"I already told you, honey. I was out walking with Snowball. I don't remember what time I left Mathers's office, but it was probably around quarter 'til eight."

"So, theoretically, someone could have poisoned the cookies between the time you left and the time I saw him on Main Street." I shook my head. "But how could someone have slipped something into the cookies with Mathers sitting right there?" I looked to Gran. "You *did* give the cookies to Mathers, right?"

"Yes. I brought them straight to his office."

"Was his assistant there?"

"No, she was coming in as I was leaving."

So much for my theory. If Monica had arrived just as Gran was leaving, she couldn't have poisoned the cookies. I sighed and returned to scanning the article. "Apparently, strychnine was banned for use in indoor pesticides, though it's still present in gopher poison."

"Gopher poison?" Gran made a face.

"I don't suppose gopher poison is the secret ingredient in your ginger cookies?"

"Why, as a matter of fact, it is. Funny that it hasn't worked on you all these years."

"Ha-ha." I rolled my eyes and racked my brain to come up with some other explanation. "I suppose with enough money, someone could have paid a technician at the lab to falsify the results. Jay Mathers's business partner certainly has the resources — and a reason to want him dead. But I just don't understand how else he could have poisoned Jay. He plays golf every morning down in Colorado Springs, and Mathers's assistant didn't mention that he'd been to see him."

For a moment, my pen hovered over Cliff Estrell's name. Then, below him, I added, *Employee with house — tax lien*. "Mathers's wife mentioned that Jay had gotten the tax lien on a property owned by one of the workers at Estrell's resort. The worker was having health issues, which was why he'd fallen behind on his property taxes."

"Oh, brother. What a great guy. You sure anyone cares that he's dead?"

"The State of Colorado certainly cares, which is why we need to figure out who did this." I chewed on the end of my pen. "Claudia said Estrell made the employee an offer on the house, but she didn't say whether they agreed to sell. If this person was in danger of losing their home, that's certainly motive to kill Mathers."

"Well, can your computer tell us which of Estrell's employees owns the house?" Gran asked.

"Maybe . . ." I was sure The Aspenwood employed hundreds, if not thousands, of people. Short of staking out the place, it was going to be tricky to figure out which one of them owned property adjacent to the resort.

I thought back to my conversation with Claudia, trying to remember any detail that could help me narrow my search. "Claudia did mention that the house was south of the fairway. And for the land to be that valuable, it would have to be right next to the resort."

Excited by this realization, I brought up a map of the

street that ran east to west along the golf course. To my surprise, there were only six houses on that block. If Claudia's information was good, I might actually be able to figure out which employee had an axe to grind with Jay Mathers.

It took me a few minutes to find the delinquent taxpayers list online — and to cross-reference that with the addresses south of the golf course. When I finally did find a match, it was as though I'd hit it big on a slot machine in Vegas. Different colored lightbulbs flashed in my head, and I could practically hear the *ding-ding-ding!*

"What is it?" asked Gran, looking up from her task of rolling fresh cookie dough into tiny little balls.

I shook my head in utter amazement. Suddenly it all made sense. "I think I know who killed Jay Mathers."

CHAPTER EIGHTEEN

The Mountain Shadow Police Department was buzzing with activity as I strode into the bullpen the next morning. In one hand, I carried an extra-large latte, while balancing a box of donuts in the other. I knew it was a little cliché, but who didn't like coffee and donuts?

I found Officer Hamby reclined in his wheely chair, one ankle crossed over the other and propped up on his desk. He was talking on the phone with a pen in hand, which he clicked as the other person talked.

He didn't notice me right away, so I had a moment to appreciate his strong, lanky frame and the way his uniform shirt hugged his biceps. The second he saw me, Hamby gave a start and abruptly slid his feet off his desk.

"I'll call you back," he said to the person on the other end of the line, a slight flush creeping into his cheeks as he replaced the receiver. "Miss McCrithers." He cleared his throat. "What can I do for you?"

I'm not sure what it was about catching Officer Handsome off guard that I found so delightful, but I couldn't help grinning as he sized me up with those gorgeous blue eyes. Remembering why I'd come, I held up the coffee and donuts. "It's more what I can do for *you*."

Officer Hamby gave me an admonishing look. "You know it's a serious crime to attempt to bribe an officer of the law." His voice was low and deep and serious, and it made my insides rumble deliciously.

"Oh, these? These aren't a bribe. Doing your job for you just makes me hungry."

Smiling sweetly, I set the coffee down on his desk and opened the box of donuts. I'd picked them up from The Filling Station, which Gran had told me made the best donuts in town. The heavenly scent of fried dough and frosting immediately made my mouth water — and, judging by the way Hamby's eyes darted into the greasy white box, he was not immune to the power of pastries.

"I know who killed Jay Mathers," I said, balancing the box on my arm and selecting a chocolate long john with sprinkles.

"Is that so?"

I nodded and took a giant bite, chewing slowly to build suspense.

Officer Hamby raised his eyebrows impatiently. "Well?"

"Oh! Help yourself," I said, holding out the box. "The coffee is for you, too. I figured caffeine was the fastest way to a cop's heart."

"Well, you're not wrong," Hamby muttered, cracking a cute lopsided grin that made my stomach flip over.

Not cute, I reminded myself. Officer Hamby was just the small-town cop who'd put Gran behind bars to save face.

"It was Roger Halliday," I said, taking another triumphant bite.

I don't know what I'd been expecting — perhaps that Officer Hamby's eyes would light up or that he'd get that staring-off-into-space look that movie cops always got when they were on the cusp of cracking a case. If I was being honest, I'd sort of hoped that Hamby would declare that I was a beautiful genius, plant a wet kiss on my mouth, and run off to tell everyone they'd gotten the wrong man — er, the wrong *gran*.

As it turned out, none of that happened. Hamby just looked confused.

"I didn't put it together when I first saw Mr. Halliday at the golf course," I said. "I thought it must have been Mathers's business partner, Cliff Estrell. But then his wife mentioned that Mathers had bought the tax lien on a property adjacent to The Aspenwood so he could gouge Estrell."

"Wait, wait, wait." Officer Hamby frowned. "You talked to Mathers's *wife*?"

"I tracked her down at the spa," I said, hoping to gloss over that little detail before Hamby could chastise me for meddling in official police business or whatever. "Anyway, I guess Estrell made Halliday an offer on his house, but Halliday refused. The place has been in his family for generations, and he didn't want to sell. At least, there's no record of that property being sold, so I assume he declined Estrell's offer. Getting rid of Mathers was the only way he could think to prevent him from going to claim the title — or maybe buy himself some time to pay back the taxes he owed. Estrell was angry that Mr. Halliday hadn't fixed his golf cart — probably because he was late coming into work last Friday because he was poisoning Jay Mathers!"

Officer Hamby just shook his head. "How do you know all this?"

I gave a modest shrug. "I paid a little visit to The Aspenwood."

"You golf?"

"No." I frowned. Why wasn't Hamby as excited as I was to learn the identity of Mathers's true killer? Maybe he was just a little slow on the uptake.

I took a bite of my donut to give him a chance to catch up. When he still didn't seem to grasp my brilliance, I said, "Strychnine might be banned for use in rat poison, but it's still used in gopher poison." And, because apparently I needed to lead the horse to water, I added, "They use gopher poison on golf courses . . ."

Suddenly the realization seemed to hit him. "Oh, you're talking about Roger Halliday, the manager at The Aspenwood golf course."

Nice work, Sherlock. He'd finally caught up — after I'd spoon-fed him the entire thing.

But Officer Hamby just shook his head. "We already looked into the owners of all the properties Mathers had secured tax liens for. The golf-course manager had an airtight alibi."

At those words, it was as if Officer Hamby had just let all the air out of my victory balloons. I could practically hear the sad whizz of air rushing out of my awesome theory.

"*What?*"

Hamby nodded. "He was having gallbladder surgery the morning Mathers was killed."

My stomach dropped. "A-are you sure?"

"Positive. I spoke with his surgeon before I stumbled upon the lien against your aunt Lucille's property."

I couldn't hide the dread that swept over my entire body. My shoulders sagged, my mouth fell open, and that familiar leaden weight sank into my gut. I was back to square one.

"I'm sorry," said Hamby. "I know how much you wanted this to be someone other than your grandmother, but —"

"She didn't do it!" I exclaimed, my dread and terror morphing into anger. "Honestly! Do you *really* think a ninety-two-year-old woman killed Jay Mathers? She was alive before they invented color TV!"

Officer Hamby's expression turned grim. "I think your grandmother is more capable and cunning than either of us gives her credit for."

"But Gran didn't have any *reason* to kill Mathers!" I exclaimed. "She was going to give me the money to pay off the taxes."

"You say that, but I did some digging into your grandmother's financial records." Officer Hamby shifted some paperwork on his desk, rifling around for something. "She has very little money besides the equity she has in her home and the family farm."

"That's not true. My grandfather worked until the day he died."

"Your grandfather was killed in an accident when he was in his sixties, right?"

I nodded.

From the mess of paperwork on his desk, Hamby produced a stack of official-looking documents with

Mountain Shadow Bank and Trust printed across the top. "My records show that your grandmother used the settlement from the railroad to pay off the home equity line of credit they'd taken out on that house. Your grandfather had life insurance, but that money has mostly gone toward your grandmother's upkeep these last thirty years."

My heart was throbbing in my throat. What Hamby was saying didn't make any sense. Why would Gran and Gramps have taken out a line of credit on their home shortly before Gramps was killed? Gran had *told* me she had plenty of money. Why would she have offered to pay the taxes on the hotel if she truly couldn't afford to?

"Listen, Caroline," said Hamby, a cold, unfeeling expression overtaking the genuine sympathy in his eyes. "I know this can be difficult to hear, but I'm only going to say it once. This investigation is official police business. You need to stay out of it."

My phone buzzed in my purse just as I was leaving the police station. I stopped on the curb to fish it out and saw that it was work.

Thinking someone from my team was calling with a question about the slide decks I'd been revising, I tapped my screen to accept the call. "This is Caroline."

"*Hey*, Caroline. It's Janine . . ."

I grimaced and held back a groan. Janine was one of those fake-sensitive types who threw around phrases like "work-life balance" and "my door is always open" while demanding that we work nights and weekends and guilting anyone who dared take a sick day.

She had this way of drawing out a person's name anytime she was calling to deliver bad news. I'd heard her use that same tone with clients a hundred times before. The fact that she was using it with me made me extremely uneasy.

"Hey, Janine," I said, trying to sound upbeat despite my nerves. "How's it going? Were you able to access the TrèsBelle slide deck all right? I made all the edits you requested."

"Oh, yes. Yes, I did find your revisions . . . I was just calling to see how vacay was going and when you were going to be back in the office. Craig needs some help getting ready for the LuckyChow presentation, and we really need all hands on deck right now."

I gritted my back teeth together and lifted my gaze to the heavens. Janine *knew* I wasn't on "vacay." She was the one who'd suggested I take some time off after I'd broken down at the pitch meeting, and I'd told her about Aunt Lucille's death. The HR-approved language around the agency was "take all the time you need to address your mental-health concerns," but when push came to shove, it was "all hands on deck."

"Oh, uh . . . I'm glad you called," I lied, careful to keep my voice light and breezy. "I wanted to talk to you about that, actually . . ."

I grimaced as I held the phone to my ear, wishing I'd had more time to think of the best way to present my request.

"Um, so I should have everything squared away with my aunt's arrangements by the end of the week. Her memorial service is on Monday . . ." I swallowed once to wet my parched throat. Janine was *never* going to go for this. "The thing is . . . my gran is having a really hard time coming to terms with her sister's death." Not to mention she was on trial for murder. "I was wondering if it would be possible for me to work remotely from Colorado for a little while? Just until she's back on her feet. You know I'm very self-directed. I can do all meetings via video conferencing, and I'd be happy to send in weekly progress reports."

There was a long, drawn-out pause. I squeezed my eyes shut and crossed all my fingers and toes.

"Mmm, *yeah*." Janine sighed in that faux-compassionate voice. "I don't think that's going to work for us."

"Oh. Okay," I choked, my throat suddenly very tight. What was I going to do? The deal R.P. had made with the court hinged on the assertion that Gran wasn't well enough to live on her own. He'd told me I needed to stay in Mountain Shadow until the trial — or else arrange live-in care, which I knew Gran couldn't afford.

But before I could pull together some persuasive argument or plead for more time off, Janine began to speak again. "You know, Caroline, if this is too much for you right now, maybe you need to rethink your priorities."

My mind was racing. What did that mean? "N-no, it's not too much for me," I added hurriedly. "You know what? Forget I said anything. If I could just take one more week to get my gran settled, I —"

Janine let out a heavy sigh. "I understand. Really, I do. It's just . . . with these new accounts, we really need everyone to have their head in the game. I think maybe this just isn't your journey right now."

A mushroom cloud of panic exploded in my chest as I frantically tried to decipher what the heck that meant.

"Oh, no!" I replied. "EightOhOne Agency is definitely my journey, and I'm so excited for the opportunity to work on the TrèsBelle and LuckyChow accounts."

"Really?" Janine asked. "Because it just doesn't seem like your heart's in it lately."

Since when? I wondered, rolling my eyes. Since I was scammed at the altar and took eight days off to deal with the death of my aunt? It wasn't as though I was asking for any special treatment, either. I had three weeks of vacation time saved up.

"I can promise you my heart's totally in it," I said, acutely aware of how desperate I sounded.

"I'm sorry, Caroline, but I need team players right now. And I think you need to focus on you."

I swallowed. "Uh . . ."

"I can offer you two months' severance, but that's the best I can do."

Two months' severance? What?

"Are you *firing* me?" My voice broke on the last word, and I clenched all my facial muscles so I didn't break down and cry.

This couldn't be happening. I was a model employee. I'd never been fired in my life!

"Don't think of it as being let go," said Janine, still in that fake-sympathetic tone that made me want to gouge her eyes out. "Think of it as re-journeying. Besides —"

I didn't hear what Janine said next. I'd already hung up the phone.

CHAPTER NINETEEN

It was with a sick feeling in my stomach that I pulled up in front of The Mountain Shadow Grand. I'd had a good cry on the drive from the police station, but I found I wasn't actually that upset about losing my job at the agency. I'd liked what I'd been doing — and it was terrifying to be out of a job — but I wasn't going to miss Janine or her sycophants.

As I let myself in the front door, the familiar musty scent of the place filled my nostrils, and the creak and groan of the scuffed parquet floor seemed to welcome me back home. It was strange, but after hallucinating about Aunt Lucille, I no longer found the hotel so creepy. Despite its leaks and cracks and creaks, I could understand why Lucille had loved the place. It was as beautiful and dramatic as she'd been in her life, and I felt a pinch of sadness in my chest when I realized I would have to sell it.

I'd blown my savings on the sham wedding, and since I was out of a job, I would need to make my severance last until I could find something else. I couldn't in good conscience allow Gran to foot the bill for Aunt Lucille's back taxes — not if Officer Hamby was right and she didn't have the money.

Oddly, it was Gran's omission that bothered me more than getting fired. Why hadn't she told me she was living on a fixed income? She certainly wasn't in the habit of hiding anything else. Unless her memory was starting to go and she didn't *realize* she was in such dire financial straits . . .

The thought made me desperately sad, and I resolved to get to the bottom of things as soon as I got home.

The floor squeaked as I shuffled across the lobby, taking the time to truly appreciate the level of craftsmanship that had gone into every detail of The Grand. Thinking I would take one last ride in Ol' Bertha, I slid the metal cage door aside and pressed the button for the third floor.

The inner cage door slid into place, and the elevator began to move. With all the windows boarded up, it was dark inside the shaft, but I could imagine riding Ol' Bertha in the hotel's heyday and watching the intricate pattern of light and shadow casting through the cage doors.

As the elevator reached the third floor, I braced myself for a little jolt, but it never came. Instead, I felt a tingle along the back of my neck as it continued to climb all the way to the fourth floor.

Bertha came to a noisy halt in front of a giant sheet of plywood, and the inner cage door retracted automatically. My stomach did an uneasy somersault, and I remembered the battered business card Rusty had given me for his elevator exorcist, which I'd left in the pocket of another pair of pants.

I sighed. If the elevator really *was* haunted, it would soon be someone else's problem.

I jabbed the button to return to the first floor, but the elevator didn't move. I hit it again, but still nothing happened.

Thinking Rusty must have missed a frayed wire or something, I tried the button for the second floor, but the elevator stayed where it was.

I tried to ignore the swell of claustrophobia in my chest as I punched the button for the third floor. Nothing. Second floor. First floor. Nothing.

Bracing my hands on the cage door, I tried desperately to think. The light above me was still on, so the elevator hadn't tripped a breaker. I hadn't felt or heard anything that would indicate a mechanical failure. It had to be a bad connection somewhere in the control panel.

I pulled out my phone to give Rusty a call, but when I tapped my screen, it stayed black.

No. My phone couldn't be dead. I couldn't have that bad of luck.

I tapped it again and even tried the button along the side, but my screen stayed dark.

As the reality of my situation began to sink in, I started to panic in earnest. I was trapped in an elevator in an abandoned hotel, and no one knew where I was.

Gran would start to worry when I didn't show up for dinner, but she wasn't allowed to leave the house. Even if she thought to send someone to look for me at The Grand, what were the chances that anyone would hear me calling from the elevator shaft three floors above? It might be a while before someone thought to check Ol' Bertha.

Pressing a hand to my chest, I tried to slow my breathing. It wouldn't do me any good to panic.

Pushing the outer cage door open, I fitted my fingers into the gap where the plywood met the wall. I could feel cool air coming through the opening, but when I braced my shoulder against the plywood, it didn't seem to want to budge. If only I had a crowbar or some kind of tool to pry it open . . .

Just then, the overhead light started to flicker and buzz. I whipped my head around — half expecting to find the ghost of Roy Wilkerson — but I was mercifully alone.

"Calm down," I told myself, letting out an uneasy laugh. "There's no — such thing — as ghosts."

"I wouldn't say that too loudly, my dear," came a voice from behind me. "Someone might take offense."

I whirled around so fast that I tweaked my neck as I came face to face with Aunt Lucille. I screamed and threw my whole body against the plywood barrier, which ripped free with a crunch. I staggered into the hallway as the plywood swung loose, righting myself against the opposite wall.

"Honestly, darling, don't you think it's time to reopen the fourth floor?" she pouted. "These were some of my *favorite* rooms."

"Wha—" The word died on my frantic exhale as I tried — and failed — to catch my breath.

Once again, Aunt Lucille was the young playbill version of herself — half see-through and black and white. She was dressed in a floor-length sheath of silk that hugged her perfect figure, and her arms were swathed in ivory-colored gloves. An enormous mink stole lay draped over her shoulders, and a ghostly cigarette smoldered from a long cigarette holder.

"You're not real," I choked. "You're not real. You're not real!"

"My dear Caroline. Haven't we been through this?"

I shook my head and edged toward the stairs, the floorboards creaking under my weight. I opened my mouth to speak and sneezed on a mote of swirling dust.

"Ghosts aren't real," I whispered.

"Real, real — what is *real*?" Lucille scoffed, throwing up her gloved hands.

I winced as a giant cherry tumbled off the end of her cigarette before remembering that it was only a figment of my imagination and couldn't burn a hole in anything.

"I'm here, aren't I? You can see me — *hear* me? I'm as real as I can be at this stage in my un-life."

I rubbed my forehead. I had to be imagining things. Aunt Lucille was simply a hallucination brought on by stress. Yes, that was it. The first time I'd seen her had been the day of Gran's arraignment, and this time I was seeing her ghost after losing my job.

But if that was true, I reasoned, then Aunt Lucille was *me*. My mind was creating her ghost based on my memories and impressions. That meant ghost Lucille couldn't possibly know anything that I didn't know myself. Asking her questions I didn't know the answer to was the fastest way to dismantle the illusion.

"Who was the first president you ever voted for?" I asked.

Lucille looked taken aback. "Franklin Roosevelt, nineteen forty-four."

"Where were you when the Japanese bombed Pearl Harbor?"

"Here at the hotel — in my room. I'd been on stage until two a.m. the night before and was *desperately* hung over."

I pressed my lips together to hold back my laugh. That certainly sounded like Aunt Lucille.

"What was the first movie you ever saw in the theatre?"

"*Cleopatra.*" She waved a hand. "Not the version with Elizabeth Taylor but the Cecil B. DeMille film."

"O-*kay* . . ." I definitely hadn't known there'd been an earlier version of that movie. I'd always assumed the Elizabeth Taylor one was the original.

My breaths were coming sharp and fast. As much as I didn't want to admit it, there was no other explanation that made sense: Aunt Lucille's ghost was real, and she was haunting my hotel.

"Are you satisfied, dear?" Lucille asked, crossing her arms over her chest and somehow managing to keep hold of that long cigarette.

I sighed. "I guess."

"Dear me. I don't think I've worked so hard for a part since I was trying to get Rhett Davis to cast me as Anna Leonowens in *The King and I*."

I bit down on the inside of my cheek. As much as it freaked me out to be talking to a ghost, it was actually nice to be able to have a conversation with my deceased great-aunt.

"Now that we're all on the same page," said Lucille, "when are you going to begin work on my beloved Grand? She is falling apart at the seams!"

My heart sank as I remembered the reason I'd returned to the hotel. I didn't want to be the one to break the news to Lucille's ghost, but if I didn't, I wasn't sure who would.

"I'm not going to be working on The Grand," I said in a quiet voice. "I can't. I'm so sorry, Aunt Lucille. But I don't have the money to pay the back taxes on this place, and I just lost my job."

Lucille's heavily penciled brows furrowed. "But what about Virginia? Surely she could lend you the money?"

I shook my head. "According to the police, Gran doesn't have the money."

"But of *course* she has the money!" Lucille let out a bark of laughter. "My sister was always the responsible one!"

"Apparently, she and Gramps took out a loan on their house before he died, and she used the settlement from the railroad company to pay it back."

At those words, something like guilt flashed in Aunt Lucille's eyes. She averted her gaze and put the end of the cigarette holder to her lips, took a puff, and blew out a delicate cloud of smoke.

"Aunt Lucille . . ."

She still didn't look at me.

I stared her down. "What aren't you telling me?"

For a long moment, Lucille didn't answer. She just gnawed on the end of her cigarette holder, looking undeniably guilty. "Oh, Caroline, you can't *possibly* understand the pressure I was under at the time! I'd met a very promising young director at a party, you see, and we'd started seeing one another. It was a bit of a May-December romance, you could say, but I was rather smitten. He confided that he was working on a *most* impressive new picture and that he was certain I would be an excellent fit for the lead. Well, you know how these things go . . ."

In truth, I didn't, but I could guess.

"The project was cursed from the very beginning. The studio demanded all sorts of rewrites." Lucille let out an indignant huff. "Well, by the time they got through with it, it was not a drama about a mature but gorgeous widow who decided to take a grand tour of Europe, but rather a romantic comedy. They wanted someone . . . well, younger. That's show business for you. The worst part was that *scoundrel* of a director dropped me like a hot potato! Looking back, I should have known that he was a fair-weather friend, I suppose, but love makes us see what we want to see."

"I don't understand," I said slowly, picking apart Aunt Lucille's story. "What does that have to do with Gran and Gramps taking out a loan?"

Lucille shot me a guilty look. "All this time, I'd been thinking I was going to get a fat payday, and instead they gave me the royal shaft. I'd leveraged my half of the farm to purchase The Grand, thinking I'd give it a bit of a spruce and be able to pay back the loan in a jiffy."

She said all of this in the breezy, matter-of-fact tone of someone who genuinely thought it had been a good idea to leverage the family farm on a gamble because some womanizing director had offered her a lucrative role.

"As you can probably guess, things did not go as planned." Lucille let out a dramatic sigh. "When I was passed over for the part, I didn't know how I was going to afford to renovate the hotel. I was able to squeak by for a while, but eventually I fell behind on the loan payments." She'd taken to chewing on the end of her thumb through her white glove, which already had a tiny hole. "Virginia and your grandfather faced a choice: Either they could buy me out to repay the loan, or we'd lose the farm."

I sucked in a breath as understanding hit me. "That's why they took out the loan on their house."

Aunt Lucille shook her head. "I wasn't sure how they managed to come up with the money. They were never wealthy people, and the sum was quite dear."

Suddenly I understood why Gran had been angry with Lucille all these years. Aunt Lucille's mistake had cost her and Gramps a fortune. Rather than coasting into their golden years with financial ease, Gramps had had to go back to work to repay the loan on their house.

"I don't understand," I said after a moment. "If you were in trouble, why didn't you sell the hotel?"

A far-off look came over Lucille as her eyes traveled over the faded floral wallpaper. "Oh, Caroline. I have so many memories of this place . . ." She heaved a sigh and smiled wanly. "After the war, your grandfather went to school on the GI Bill, and Virginia came out here to stay with me." Lucille's smile warmed. "She and I launched our act in the ballroom downstairs."

My mouth fell open, and I gaped at Aunt Lucille. "You and Gran had an *act*?"

She nodded. "It was short-lived, but it was one of the best seasons of my life. Ginger and I spent every day together. We didn't have much money, but when the weather was nice, we used to walk down to the penny arcade and drink cherry sodas. At night, we'd do our act. For a while, we went on the road. I don't think I ever had so much fun performing with anyone as I did with my sister. When your grandfather finished school, she sold her dancing shoes at a thrift store and got married. But I will never forget those years." She shook her head. "I guess I just couldn't let it go."

Lucille didn't say it, but I knew the sacrifices she'd made. Gran and Gramps might have bailed her out, but Lucille had spent the last years of her life in that awful nursing home rather than sell The Grand.

"I know how it must sound," said Aunt Lucille. "But you must understand how much I loved Virginia. All my life, I was married to the theatre, and the silver screen was my mistress. I never had a family of my own, and after Mother and Daddy died, Ginger was all I had." She let out another heavy sigh. "Oh, Caroline, we simply *must* find a way to make this right! I know your grandmother will never forgive me, but if we lose the hotel after all these years, it will all have been for nothing!"

I opened my mouth to tell Lucille that I was out of ideas, but her mistress comment had sparked something in my memory.

Claudia Mathers had said her husband had been seeing the woman who worked for him. I'd assumed she'd been talking about his assistant, Monica, but Claudia had mentioned something about long blond hairs in the shower drain. Monica was brunette, so it couldn't have been her.

My mind raced as Lucille continued to fret. What if Jay Mathers hadn't just been cheating on his wife? What if he'd been two-timing Claudia *and* his assistant and Monica had found out about it? That would certainly have given her a motive. I still didn't know how she could have poisoned Mathers, but I intended to find out.

"I-I have to go," I stammered, cutting off Lucille midsentence.

She blinked at me, looking offended that I'd interrupted her treatise on the bonds of sisterhood.

"I'm sorry," I spluttered. "But this is urgent. I think I just figured it out!"

"You know how to save the hotel?" she asked.

"No," I said, heading for the stairs. "But I might have an idea who killed Jay Mathers!"

CHAPTER TWENTY

Less than five minutes later, I was storming up the steps to Jay Mathers's office — prepared to burst through the door to confront Monica. I couldn't go to the police — not until I figured out how she'd done it and had some rock-solid evidence to present to Officer Hamby.

The door was locked, but I could see a light on in the front room, and there was a silver Camry parked on the street that I would have bet my hotel belonged to Monica. I rapped on the glass, but no one answered, so I just knocked harder.

It took nearly a minute of steady banging, but Monica finally came to the door. Her expression darkened when she saw me standing there, but she reached down to unlock the deadbolt.

While she was distracted, I reached into my purse and hit "record" on my phone's recorder app in case I managed to elicit a confession.

"I know you lied," I blurted as soon as she opened the

door. "I know you brought Mr. Mathers his coffee the morning he was killed."

Monica's face seemed to drain of all color, and for a second I thought she might slam the door in my face. Instead, she sucked in a breath, pursed her lips, and stepped aside to let me through the door.

For two heartbeats, I stood frozen on the landing. I'd expected her to deny my accusation, and instead she was inviting me in?

What if Monica really *was* the killer? It didn't seem smart to be having this conversation in the privacy of an empty office building. But then I thought of Gran and how small she'd looked the morning of her arraignment. If I went to Officer Hamby, it would give Monica a chance to get her story straight and destroy any evidence of her crime. I couldn't let that happen.

Taking a deep breath, I stepped inside. The window AC unit was turned on full-blast, and goosebumps sprang up all over my body.

"Tell me what you think you know," said Monica as soon as she'd closed the door behind me.

"I know you went to Déjà Brew on Friday morning to pick up Mathers's usual order."

"That's true," she murmured, her voice strangely calm. "But I didn't poison him."

"Not with the coffee," I said. "The medical examiner's report showed that he didn't have anything besides cookies in his stomach." I crossed my arms over my chest to hide my shaking hands. "So how did you do it?"

"Do what?" she asked.

I took a deep breath. "How did you slip him the poison?"

"I didn't," said Monica in a wounded voice. "He didn't have any coffee in his stomach because I didn't give him his drink." She looked down at the floor, cheeks burning. "But I did lie about seeing him that morning."

Suddenly I wished I'd tested the whole voice-recorder-in-the-purse setup to be sure I captured everything she said. I honestly hadn't expected Monica to come right out and confess to her crime. It would be just my luck to lose it all because of some technical issue.

"Tell me what happened," I said quietly.

Monica let out a shaky sigh. "Friday morning, I came into the office really early to print out an agreement we'd drawn up the day before. Jay likes to have any important documents on his desk for review when he gets in at eight." Her face crumpled slightly then, as if she'd only just remembered that her boss was dead. "Just before seven, I picked up coffee at Déjà Brew and went straight to his place, like I always do."

Monica broke off and glanced at me, so I nodded for her to continue.

"He was there, but he wasn't alone." She swallowed thickly at the memory, tears welling up in her eyes.

"Was Mrs. Mathers there?"

Monica shook her head. "Claudia I could have handled. She and Jay hadn't . . . Well, there was nothing between them anymore, and I'm pretty sure she knew that Jay and I were seeing each other." Her bottom lip trembled, and a fat tear slid down her cheek. "It was Julia, the woman who scouted properties for him." Monica looked back down at the floor. "I hadn't seen that coming."

"And were the two of them . . . sleeping together?" I asked as gently as I could.

Monica nodded, tears streaming silently down her cheeks. "I was stupid to think I was the only one he was seeing, but . . ." She sniffed and wiped a hand under her eyes. "It just took me by surprise."

I nodded, chewing on the inside of my lip. While Monica might have gotten what she deserved, I could imagine it would have been quite the shock to realize the two-timer was two-timing her.

"I was so embarrassed," she whispered, so softly I almost didn't hear it. "I-I didn't know what to do, so I just turned around and left. I didn't even give him his coffee."

"Well, considering the circumstances, I'd say he didn't deserve a latte."

A bubble of teary laughter burst out of Monica, but then she started sobbing in earnest. "How could he *do* this to me?" she wailed. "I did *everything* for that man! I picked up his dry-cleaning. I ordered his groceries. I picked up his dog's heartworm medicine . . . ordered the chemicals for his hot tub. I even shopped for his wife's birthday presents!"

Oh boy. I gave an inward cringe. She'd had it *bad*.

I couldn't understand what would motivate a woman like Monica to give her heart to a man she could never have, but I still felt bad for her. She might have been sleeping with someone else's husband, but Mathers's flagrant abuse of power and the way he'd led her on made him just as scummy as Todd.

"What happened after you left Mr. Mathers's house?" I asked once Monica's sniffles had subsided.

She dragged in a shaky breath. "Usually, I get back to the office to answer the phone and get things organized before Jay arrives, but . . ." She shook her head, and her face crumpled in a wave of fresh sobs. "I couldn't face him after that, you know? So I just drove around for a while, trying to clear my head . . ."

"And when you got to the office, you saw my gran leaving?"

Monica nodded. "I don't think Jay wanted to see me any more than I wanted to see him. He was in his office when I got here, so I grabbed the documents I needed to mail and left for the post office. I never saw him again." Monica's voice cracked on the last few words, and she looked up at the ceiling to try to stop her tears.

"I'm sorry," I said. Monica might have brought all this heartbreak on herself, but I still felt sorry for her.

I honestly didn't think she'd killed her boss. Everything she'd said fit with what I knew of the case. Unfortunately, she hadn't given me any information that might help exonerate Gran.

"I don't mean to be insensitive, but . . . do you think this Julia woman might have killed him?"

Monica swallowed and shook her head. "Why would she? Jay paid her a commission on every property she found that the company bought. With him gone, she's out of a job just like everyone else."

I nodded, turning that over in my head. Even if this Julia had been worried about people finding out about her relationship with Mathers, I didn't see how she could have poisoned him.

"Please don't tell the cops I lied," Monica pleaded. "I was hurt and angry, but I *swear* I didn't kill him."

"I believe you," I said, shivering as the window AC unit kicked on again — blasting me with a wave of frigid air. "How do you *stand* working in here?" I asked through chattering teeth. "It's freezing!"

"Sorry," she said. "I guess I'm just used to it."

I wanted to point out that she was also wearing a turtleneck sweater in the middle of July, but I just watched in silence as she crossed the room to turn down the AC. The cold air carried the scent of drywall and fresh paint, and I remembered that the office had been undergoing renovations the first time I'd visited.

"Does this building not have central AC?" I asked.

Monica shook her head. "Old building. Jay decided not to install a new HVAC system, since you only need AC a few months out of the year."

"Is there a window unit back there as well?" I asked, hitching a thumb toward the office door, which was still blocked off with crime-scene tape.

Monica nodded.

"Did Mr. Mathers have the AC on when you came in that morning?"

Monica frowned. "I . . . don't remember. He probably did. His window faces east, so it's hot in there in the mornings."

My mind was racing. I didn't know how it all fit together, but I felt sure that I was onto something. "And did you leave the office unlocked when you left to get the coffee?"

The question came out sharper than I'd intended, and Monica gave a guilty cringe. "It's a small town," she said quietly. "I planned on coming right back after I dropped off Jay's order."

So anyone could have come in and out in the time Monica had been gone.

As I ran through all the research I'd done on strychnine poisoning, I had the sudden feeling of something sliding into place.

Strychnine takes the form of a bitter crystalline powder that is completely odorless.

Wandering over to Monica's desk, I reached down and swiped a finger across the surface. It came away with a thin layer of white drywall dust.

"It's been a job keeping the dust down with all the remodeling," she said in an apologetic tone.

I rubbed the fine white powder between my fingers, thinking hard. "Has anyone run the AC in the back office since Mr. Mathers was killed?"

"No." Monica shook her head. "The police turned it off when they got here so it didn't disturb any trace evidence."

Suddenly I had a thought. What if the poison hadn't come from something Mathers had ingested, but rather something he'd *inhaled*?

If the strychnine powder had been hidden in Mathers's window AC unit, it would explain how Gran's cookies had tested positive for the poison. If they'd been sitting on his desk when the AC kicked on, the cookies and the plate would have been *covered*. And with all the drywall dust, a little strychnine powder on the desk would have gone unnoticed.

"What?" Monica asked.

I realized I must have been staring off into space and quickly refocused on the conversation we'd been having. "I think I know how he was poisoned, and it wasn't my gran's cooking."

I scrambled for the door, nearly tripping over my own

feet in my haste to share my theory with Officer Hamby. Halfway out, I remembered Monica and turned back to shout, "Whatever you do, *don't* turn on that air conditioning!"

"It was in the air conditioner!" I huffed at Officer Hamby, cornering him by the Xerox machine and struggling to catch my breath.

Hamby froze with his hand still in the printer tray, glancing behind me as though he expected the kindly receptionist to come remove me from the building. "Miss McCrithers," he said, frowning slightly. "You're back."

I had to admit, I was a little put-out that he didn't look happy to see me. Perhaps I should have been embarrassed to face Hamby after my last theory had gone up in smoke, but I was too desperate to feel any shame. Gran's freedom hinged on me getting to the bottom of this, and I was determined to convince Hamby that her cookies hadn't been the cause of Mathers's death.

"Call me Caroline," I said. "Look, I know my theory about Roger Halliday didn't pan out, but I think you'll find that if you swab the front grill of the window AC unit in Jay Mathers's office, you'll find traces of strychnine."

Hamby's eyebrows shot up, and he seemed to forget about whatever he'd been waiting to retrieve from the copier. I had a sudden image of him grabbing me around the middle and hoisting me up onto the copier to fulfill all of my wildest fantasies involving an office Xerox machine. Instead, he just frowned.

"Well, that fits," he said, running a hand through his short blond hair.

"It *does*?" I hadn't expected him to accept my theory so readily — not after I'd struck out on my first big reveal.

Hamby nodded. "After you stormed in here accusing Halliday of murder, it got me thinking . . . Your gran might have had motive, means, and opportunity, but she wasn't the only one."

"No?" I asked, allowing myself to feel cautiously optimistic.

Hamby glanced around again. "You didn't hear it from me, but I'm going to be bringing the assistant in for questioning. Turns out she was seeing Mathers, and Mathers had another mistress on the side. Monica Lafnagle was in the office the morning he was killed, so she had motive *and* opportunity."

I blinked stupidly at Officer Hamby. Did this mean they were going to be dropping the charges against Gran?

"Credit-card transactions show that Mathers's assistant placed an order with LawnNPool, an online retailer that sells gopher poison containing strychnine. I'm still waiting for an itemized invoice detailing exactly what Miss Lafnagle ordered, but I'm fairly confident she bought the stuff with the intention of poisoning her boss."

My stomach twisted. Poor Monica. Just as I'd dismissed all the red flags with Todd, she'd seen what she wanted to see in Mathers, and she'd been burned. Now she was about to be charged with murder, when all she'd done was cater to the man's every need.

"It wasn't her," I blurted before I could stop myself. As much as I wanted to get Gran off the hook, I wasn't going to let some innocent woman go down for murder.

Hamby raised his eyebrows. "How do you know?"

"I-I just . . . *do*."

I hastily gave Officer Hamby a play-by-play of the morning according to Monica. He looked as though he wanted to chastise me for visiting her in the first place, but he kept his mouth shut and listened to the entire tale with rapt attention. His frown deepened when I got to the part about Monica fleeing with Mathers's coffee, but when I finished, I could tell I hadn't done anything to change his mind.

"That's a really nice story, but it doesn't change the fact that the woman had motive *and* opportunity. She could easily have lured him away from his desk and poisoned the cookies while he wasn't looking."

"She didn't kill Mathers!" I spluttered. "She was in *love* with him. She did everything for that man — all his errands. She even bought his wife presents and ordered the stuff for his hot tub! *That's* probably what she got from LawnNPool!"

Hamby gave an exasperated sigh. "Look, I believe that this woman might have loved Mathers, but it doesn't mean she didn't kill him. In any case, we have enough to charge her. I thought you'd be happy, since it looks as though your gran's gonna get off."

I let out a huff. "It wasn't her."

"Don't take this the wrong way, Caroline, but when you've been doing this for a while, you learn not to believe every sob story you hear."

His voice was harsh, and the implication that I was some naive Mary Sue stung more than I wanted to admit. I glared back at Hamby, certain he was wrong but too mad to come up with some other explanation.

"You're not a cop, Caroline," he said, sweeping his papers out of the printer tray and fixing me with his steely blue gaze. "Stay out of this, or next I'll be charging you with obstruction of justice."

CHAPTER TWENTY-ONE

Raindrops pelted the grimy glass pane as I stared out the window of Aunt Lucille's favorite room. The sky was an overcast steely gray, and although it was only late afternoon, Phantom Canyon Boulevard was dark and gloomy.

After leaving the station, my first impulse had been to run home and tell Gran the good news that they would likely be dropping the charges against her, but I hadn't been able to bring myself to do it. For one thing, I didn't want to get her hopes up. Once Hamby realized that Monica hadn't killed her boss, we would be right back where we started with Gran as the number-one suspect. I needed to identify the actual killer to make sure she was in the clear.

I was also dreading the conversation I knew we needed to have about why Gran had lied to me about her finances. Her money situation wasn't really my business, but since my dad — her son — was dead, there was no one else to look out for her.

So I'd driven back to The Mountain Shadow Grand and was bouncing ideas off of Aunt Lucille's ghost. Either this was an opportunity for me to reconnect with my great-aunt from beyond the grave, or I'd finally succumbed to insanity.

"Let's just run through it again, darling. I'm sure there must be *some* detail we've overlooked!"

I shook my head and leaned my forehead against the cool, dusty windowpane. "We've been over every one of the potential suspects, and I still don't know who did it."

Aunt Lucille's ghost had shed her silk evening gown and was now wearing a long-sleeve off-the-shoulder number with a simple diamond choker. She was reclined on the canopy bed in her stocking feet with one leg stacked on top of the other. Desmond was stretched out beside her on the musty old mattress, one paw resting on Lucille's exposed calf.

"Perhaps if we had a visual representation of all the suspects and the evidence, something would jump out at us," she mused.

"You mean, like, a murder board?"

"Yes, exactly! A *murder board*!" Lucille sat up and clapped her hands excitedly. "Ooh, this is so fun! I always wanted to play an old gumshoe detective on the silver screen, but those parts were always for men. I was only ever cast as Betsy Laponte — the beautiful femme fatale who caught the eye of both the police detective and the private eye before luring them both to their deaths!"

I snorted and cast around the room. While nineteenth-century hotels were big on textured wallpaper, crystal light fixtures, and sky-high ceilings, they were certainly lacking in office supplies. Luckily, I always traveled with an abundance of sticky notes and my own dry-erase markers — a habit I'd picked up working at the ad agency.

"I have an idea," I said, snatching one of the grubby old sheets that had been covering up the furniture and using it to wipe the grime off the inside of the window. I uncapped a pink marker, laid out my Filofax, and started copying the list of suspects from my planner onto the window itself.

Beside each person, I wrote his or her motive. Since Claudia had been out of the country at the time of the murder and Roger Halliday had been undergoing gallbladder surgery, I drew a line through both their names.

When I'd finished my list, I stood back and admired my handiwork. I didn't think Officer Hamby could have done any better.

Monica (assistant) - jealous rage?
~~Claudia (wife) - cheating husband, divorce, inheritance~~
Cliff Estrell (business partner) - betrayed by Mathers
Bellamy Broussard (B&B owner) - wanted Mountain Shadow Grand
~~Roger Halliday (golf course manager) - tax lien on house~~

"Why isn't Virginia on the list?" asked Aunt Lucille after a moment.

I turned and fixed her with a look. "We're trying to prove Gran *didn't* do it."

"But what if she did do it?" Lucille asked. "A good detective considers all the possibilities, and it would be *très noir* if it turned out that Virginia did kill him."

"Fine," I sighed, fighting the jab of betrayal as I wrote:
Gran — tax lien, money problems?

With my pad of lavender sticky notes, I jotted down what we knew of the case so far:

Victim had only eaten the ginger cookies that morning — no coffee

Poison transmitted through air conditioning?

Time of death: 8:15ish

Poisoning occurred between 7:15 and 8:00

Monica present at Mathers's home and office

Gran at office

Office door left unlocked

I clustered my sticky notes beside the list of suspects and stood back to take it all in. "The problem is it could have been any one of them," I muttered. "*Anyone* could have slipped into Mathers's office after Monica left and tampered with the air conditioning. Or I suppose *she* could have done it."

"But how would they have gotten the poison?" asked Lucille. "I thought you said it was banned."

"It was banned for use in indoor pesticides." I capped my pen and tapped the end against my lower lip. "My first thought was the gopher bait, but I did a little research, and I think the poison would need to be more concentrated to poison him through inhalation."

"Where would one get such a thing?"

"I don't know." I didn't think any of the suspects would be foolish enough to order strychnine over the internet from The Poison Barn, if such a website existed.

"That Bellamy Broussard," Aunt Lucille mused. "Now he is *really* something."

I frowned at Bellamy's name on the window. "How do you mean?"

"Oh, he came to visit me at Sunnyview to make me an offer on The Grand." Lucille snorted. "Of course I sent him packing. He thought he was going to scoop up the hotel for a song just because I was a frail old lady. But I'm no fool. I wouldn't have given up this place for all the tea in China — *certainly* not for what he was offering!"

I smiled at the thought of Aunt Lucille sending the pompous B&B owner away.

Not for all the tea in China.

For some reason, that phrase stuck with me. It had a nice ring to it, but there was something else — a feeling of unease I couldn't quite shake.

I stared through our list of names, out the window at the rain-soaked street. Across from the hotel, I saw a figure moving under the streetlight. It was Gideon, the bartender, taking a load of garbage out to the dumpster.

"That building," I murmured, tapping the glass. "Mathers bought it just before he was killed."

"So?"

"So he planned on tearing the whole thing down and putting up some six-story mixed-use building. Now that Mathers is dead, that's not going to happen."

That was good news for just about everybody in town, if the new building was going to be the eyesore Bellamy Broussard claimed. That was why he'd tried to get it designated as a local landmark. It didn't make sense for him to go to all that trouble if he'd known Mathers would soon be dead.

I supposed if Mathers had torn down the building with the bar, Gideon would have been out of a job. But he seemed like the sort of person who could get a job just about anywhere, and a small-town bartending gig was hardly motive for murder.

No. The person who'd killed Jay Mathers had either

been confident that they wouldn't get caught, or else they'd felt that they had nothing to lose.

Who else benefitted if Mathers's project fell through? Certainly it made no difference to the owner of the building. He'd gotten his money through the sale. But —

I sucked in a sharp breath as the realization hit me.

All this time, I'd assumed the proprietor of the tea shop owned the building across the street, but Bellamy Broussard had told me the owner was a woman.

"What is it, dear?" asked Lucille.

"I think I've got it," I whispered.

I flipped to the very back of my Filofax, where I'd stuffed the research I'd printed out at Gran's. As I scanned the text, the information I'd been seeking practically leapt off the page.

Strychnine is an alkaloid derived from the plant Strychnos nux-vomica, *which is native to the tropical forests in Sri Lanka, Indonesia, and Southern India.*

All my blood seemed to pool at my feet. How had I not put it together before? There was one person who stood to benefit from Mathers's death who wasn't on my list — someone who'd had not just a motive, but the means and opportunity, as well.

Aunt Lucille was as white as a sheet when I finally looked up from my research. "I think I know who the killer is."

"I NEED to speak to Officer Hamby," I said, plunking my hands down on the front desk of the police station and leaning close to the plexiglass divider. "It's about the Jay Mathers murder investigation."

"I'm afraid the detective is in an interview," said the kindly receptionist, her voice courteous but firm.

I shook my head. "I know he thinks Mathers's assistant did it, but Monica Lafnagle is innocent."

The receptionist pursed her lip, looking torn. "That sounds important."

"It is," I sighed, relieved she understood.

I could tell she wasn't used to bending the rules, and conflict warred in the receptionist's eyes as she picked up the telephone, dialed an extension, and held up a finger for me to wait. A familiar voice answered on the fifth ring, though it was too quiet for me to tell who it was.

"Hi, detective. It's Marge. There's a young lady here to see Officer Hamby." Marge glanced up at me. "She says she has pertinent information regarding the Jay Mathers case."

There was a long pause as she listened, nodding attentively and making little "hmm" sounds.

"Uh-huh. I *see*. Uh-huh. Okay. Yes, I'll tell her. Thank you, detective. Uh-huh. Buh-bye." Marge hung up the phone and turned to me with a sympathetic expression. "I just spoke to Detective Pierce, Officer Hamby's partner."

"And?"

Marge's carefully penciled eyebrows lifted. "Apparently they've just had a break in the case."

"They *have*?" I would have been surprised if Officer Hamby had come to the same conclusion I had, but maybe he was smarter than I gave him credit for.

Marge nodded. "I guess they've made an arrest."

"Who?"

She opened her mouth and closed it again, glancing around conspiratorially. "I shouldn't say, but I do know that Officer Hamby was in interrogation with the victim's assistant for over an hour."

I let out a heavy sigh. "It — wasn't — *her*! If I could just talk to Hamby, I know I could —"

At that moment, I heard a door down the adjacent hallway snick shut and the rumble of low male voices. I recognized one of the speakers at once as Officer Hamby.

"Officer Hamby!" I called, bypassing Marge to shoot down the hallway. I managed to corner Hamby and Detective Pierce in the middle of what appeared to be an intense conversation. The two of them looked up at the sound of my voice, and for a second I thought Hamby might turn and run in the other direction. Detective Pierce looked amused.

"Miss McCrithers," said Hamby in his best impression of a stern cop voice.

I decided to ignore the "Miss McCrithers" business and get straight to the point. "I think I know who really killed Jay Mathers," I said. "I just need you to check on Dana Marzetti. I'm sure if you checked his credit-card statements, you'd see that he was in India just before Mathers was killed."

"Give it a rest, McCrithers," said Hamby in a tired voice. "We just arrested Mathers's assistant and charged her with first-degree murder."

"She didn't do it!" I spluttered, still breathless from all the excitement. "Even if they were having an affair, why would she kill the man who signed her checks?"

"Monica Lafnagle admitted to being at the victim's home the morning he was killed. She was the last person to see Mathers before he left the office. She had access to his food — his air conditioner, if your theory turns out to be correct — *and* she was angry when she discovered he was having another affair."

"But she'd only learned of the affair that morning," I protested. "How would she have had time to rustle up some poison between seven and eight o'clock?"

Hamby's blue eyes locked on to mine. "She may have told you she only learned of the affair that day, but Mathers has charges on his credit card for motel rooms going back at least three months. Do you *really* think the woman who paid his bills and brought him his coffee was in the dark that long?"

I opened my mouth and then closed it again. Hamby had a point, but then Aunt Lucille's words rose to the surface of my mind: Love makes us see what we want to see.

I couldn't explain it, but I just knew that Monica hadn't killed her boss. She'd been too broken up about his death the first time I'd gone to see her to have murdered him in cold blood.

"If you'd just listen to me —"

"I'm sorry, Caroline," said Officer Hamby in a tone of cold finality. "But I've heard enough of your theories. Unless you have proof that exonerates Miss Lafnagle, I'm afraid I'm gonna have to ask you to leave."

CHAPTER TWENTY-TWO

As I pulled up in front of Chumley's, I could hear Sam Cooke blaring from inside the bar. A few cars were parked in the cramped lot behind the building, but World's Cup Tearoom and Emporium looked deserted.

Desmond rode in the passenger seat beside me, his eerie yellow eyes flashing in the glow of the streetlamp as the Pinto inched around the block. I circled the building at a crawl, looking for security cameras and not finding any.

I came to a halt on the side farthest from Main Street, parked the car, and killed the engine. Rifling around on the floorboard, I found the little paper bag I'd gotten from the hardware store and dug out the set of Allen wrenches. I tucked them into the pocket of Gran's trench coat, along with a flashlight I'd found in the glove box.

While my top concern was keeping Gran out of jail, I couldn't let an innocent woman go down for murder — not when the real killer was right across the street from The Mountain Shadow Grand.

Hamby needed proof? I intended to find that proof, clear Gran's name, and free Monica while I was at it.

"Stay here and keep a lookout," I told Desmond.

Only his huge yellow eyes were visible in the dark. At my suggestion, they narrowed into slits, and he let out a petulant *ree-ow*.

"You don't like the rain anyway," I reasoned, opening the car door and stepping out into the cold evening drizzle.

Pulling up the collar of Gran's coat, I crossed the sidewalk in two brisk strides, discreetly searching the dark windows for any signs of life. I was sure I looked incredibly suspicious, but the side street was deserted.

No one had bothered replacing the seldom-used back door of the tearoom, which was lucky, since I was a novice lock-picker. Kneeling down on the crumbling asphalt, I carefully inserted one Allen wrench and wriggled it up until I felt it catch on the lever inside the lock. At first the wrench slipped unexpectedly, and I had to try a few more times until I was able to hold it in place.

Heart pounding, I slid another wrench into the keyhole. I twisted, but it wouldn't budge, and I worried my wrench might break off in the lock. But then I heard a little *click* and felt the deadbolt move back.

"Yes!" I whispered, simultaneously flabbergasted and highly impressed with myself that I'd actually managed to pick the lock.

Tossing one last glance over my shoulder, I slipped inside and pulled the door closed behind me until it was loosely wedged in the jamb. On the off chance that there *was* someone inside the building, I didn't want to alert them to my presence by forcing the old door closed.

The cloying stench of incense was the first thing that hit me as I entered the tearoom, but the more subtle earthy aroma of tea came second. The spindly outlines of tables and chairs loomed in the artificial light from the streetlamp, and the gold statue of Ganesha gleamed eerily from his spot by the windows.

Careful not to turn on my flashlight where it could be seen from the street, I felt my way over to the counter and found a door leading to some kind of storeroom. The scent of tea was stronger in there, and I pulled out my light and shined it around the space.

I was standing in a cramped, narrow room lined with tall metal shelves. Dusty tea kettles stood like so many tin soldiers along the top shelf, while the lower shelves were crammed with brown paper packages that must have been full of loose-leaf tea.

To my right was a battered desk, and the wall behind it was full of compartments with little sliding wooden doors. I went first to the desk and began rifling through a stack of receipts. If I could find an invoice or something that placed Dana in India in the weeks preceding Jay Mathers's murder, I might be able to prove he'd had access to the poison.

As the wonderful floral aroma of tea wafted around me, I found myself questioning whether the soft-spoken teashop owner could really have killed Jay Mathers.

I hadn't put it together until Aunt Lucille's comment about all the tea in China. That was when I'd remembered that Dana had mentioned he'd just returned from India. The Nilgiri tea he'd offered me and Gran came from the Blue Mountains, which were part of the Ghat mountain range that stretched across Southern India.

Strychnos nux-vomica also grew in that region, and the seeds of that tree contained more strychnine than what was commercially available in the United States. It would have been easy for Dana to smuggle the seeds back in any of his packets of tea. I just needed proof he'd done it.

Unfortunately, all the papers on his desk were printed in either Japanese or Mandarin. There was nothing placing him in India in the days leading up to the murder.

Next I slid open the door to the largest compartment above the desk. The cubby was full of old tea strainers, stacks of cups, and cracked teapots. I made quick work of all the cupboards, but apart from a stack of mail containing an unopened jury duty slip, I didn't find anything incriminating.

Frustrated, I snapped the last cupboard door shut. I'd been so sure that Dana was the killer. He rented the unit in the building where the tearoom was located, which meant that Mathers's plans to demolish the structure would have threatened his entire business. The front window of the tearoom had a clear view of Mathers's office building across the street, which meant Dana would have seen Monica leave and had plenty of time to plant the poison in the vents of Mathers's window AC.

"Looking for something?"

The voice behind me made my whole body jerk, and as I wheeled around to face the intruder, my stomach dropped to my knees.

Dana Marzetti was standing just inside the entrance to the storeroom. I couldn't see his face in the dim light cast by the single hanging bulb, but the light coming in through the windows behind him illuminated the shape of his distinctive round glasses.

"Uh . . ." My heart was pounding so loudly I was sure Dana could hear it. "I was just —"

"I know what you were doing." Dana's voice was sharp, but he didn't sound nearly as angry as I would have expected for finding an intruder in his shop. "Word gets around, you know. I've heard you've been asking a lot of questions about Jay Mathers's death."

I swallowed, and my throat felt as though it were covered in a thousand tiny paper cuts. What were the odds that I'd be able to talk my way out of this one? I couldn't think of any plausible explanation for why I'd been poking around in the tearoom, so I decided to go with the truth and hope that I could convince Dana that I'd put my suspicions to rest.

"I'm sorry," I said, hoping the strained sound of my voice might pass for embarrassment. "I don't know what I was thinking."

Dana didn't say a word, and his silence terrified me more than if he'd shouted.

"I-I was following a hunch, and I got a little carried away." I shook my head and tried to draw a full breath. "I'm so sorry for intruding. I don't know what's gotten into me."

I forced an uneasy chuckle, wishing I could see Dana's expression to know whether he'd bought my act. But Dana didn't move into the light. He just continued to stare at me through those thick round glasses.

"And what was your hunch?" he asked softly. He sounded curious but not amused — like a killer wanting to make sure he'd covered his tracks.

"Oh . . . you're gonna laugh when I tell you," I said.

Dana waited in excruciating silence.

I gave a theatrical sigh. "I thought you'd brought back *strychnos nux-vomica* seeds from your travels and used them to poison Jay Mathers." I threw up my hands in a helpless gesture. "I thought he'd inhaled the poison through his window AC unit. It would have explained how the strychnine crystals ended up on my gran's cookies when there wasn't any poison in the rest of the batch." I swallowed to wet my parched throat. "I feel pretty silly now."

Dana made a little "hmmph" sound in his throat. At first I thought he might let me go with a cold warning, but then he began to speak. "The wonderful thing about owning a teashop is that it allows me to travel to the most remote villages to find the very best teas. During my time in this business, I have had the privilege of meeting the most astounding array of people from all walks of life."

He took a step closer, and a beam of yellowish light fell across his face. "I once met a farmer in Tamil Nadu who was so poor he was struggling to feed his nine children and his wife's aging parents. He had been forced to mortgage his tiny plot of farmland, and yet he was the kindest, most generous person that I have ever met." A cold look flashed through Dana's eyes, and his expression hardened. "Jay Mathers is a man who has *everything*, and yet he is one of the most selfish, cold-hearted people I have ever known."

I didn't know what to say to that. Given the circumstances, "good riddance" didn't seem appropriate.

"I have dedicated my life to preserving the old ways of drinking tea, appropriate to the plant and the culture from which it comes," said Dana. "Jay Mathers was the antithesis of that. He sought only to destroy. He bought this building so that he could demolish it and turn it into condominiums and offices. He didn't care about the history that would be lost or the lives that would be ruined — he only cared that it would be profitable."

Dana took another step forward, and my skin itched with the realization that he was completely blocking my exit.

"I went to him, you know," Dana said softly. "*Pleaded* with him to sell the building. I offered him twenty thousand more than he'd paid for it, but he wouldn't sell. He just laughed in my face and told me he stood to make millions on the development." A manic look flashed through Dana's eyes as he added, "I've been here for twenty years. I went to his office to speak with him several times, and each time he would lean back in that leather chair with the air conditioner blowing on him like that, and he'd sneer at me like I was nothing."

Dana's nostrils flared at the memory. "It took me a while to learn how to process the strychnine from the seeds, but once I did, I knew exactly how I would poison him. I knew that by the time anyone learned what was wrong with him, he would be beyond saving. I hadn't planned on your grandmother going to visit him that morning. I was merely relieved that she had not been poisoned. I am truly sorry that the two of you had to get caught up in this mess."

At those words, my heart felt as though it might punch right out of my chest. The room suddenly felt much too small. Dana reached into the breast pocket of his jacket, and I took an automatic step back. My legs collided with the desk behind me just as Dana produced a tiny snub-nosed revolver.

"I regret that it has to come to this," he said, pointing the gun at my chest. "Mathers deserved to die a slow, miserable death, but you don't. I promise that your death will be much, much quicker."

CHAPTER TWENTY-THREE

As Dana held the revolver on me, time seemed to slow down. The tall shelves loomed like a tunnel around us, and all my attention focused on Dana and the gun.

"You *were* breaking and entering," said Dana, almost to himself. "I will have shot you in self-defense." His voice shook a little on the last few words, but he drew in a sharp breath and nodded. "There's not a jury in the world that would convict me."

My heart was beating so loudly that I barely heard him. Then, out of the corner of my eye, I saw a flicker of movement along one of the shelves. At first I thought I'd imagined it, or that I'd only seen a shadow. But then something dark shimmered above me, and I caught a flash of yellow eyes.

Desmond leapt from the shelf with a loud *yee-ow,* and I only had a split second to process what was happening as he arched toward Dana's outstretched arm. His claws snagged on a patch of bare skin, and Dana let out a roar of pain.

The revolver clattered to the floor as Dana threw back his arm, tossing Desmond off him. I didn't think. I just dove for the gun as Desmond's yowl filled my ears.

Sprawling across the filthy tile, I watched in horror as the gun skittered over the floor and slid underneath the shelves. Before I could reach for it, I caught a flash of movement, and Dana slammed down on top of me.

A sharp cry tore from my throat as he thrust his elbow into my ribs. He flipped me over onto my back, eyes bulging behind his glasses as sweaty fingers groped for my neck.

Ree-ow!

Out of the corner of my eye, I saw Desmond leap onto Dana's back, digging in his long sharp claws. Dana's weight lifted momentarily as he jerked back, throwing Desmond to the ground and sending him streaking behind a shelf.

Panic seized me as Dana's fingers dug into my windpipe, cutting off the flow of oxygen. Desperately I tried to peel his hands away, but Dana clung on despite my flailing.

As blackness pressed in around the corners of my vision, I was overwhelmed by the force of my rage. I was angry with Hamby and furious with Todd, but mostly I was angry with myself.

I hadn't come to the tearoom to get proof for Hamby. I'd come to confirm my own suspicions.

After being played the fool back in Chicago and destroying my credibility with the handsome policeman, I no longer trusted my own instincts. I'd needed to know without a shadow of a doubt that Dana was the true killer.

Now he was going to kill *me*.

As I sank deeper into the darkness, my fury seeped into the ground around me. I could feel it vibrating in my bones and the floor where I lay — the ground trembling with the force of my rage.

Literally, I could *feel* the earth moving — gently at first, like the rumble from a passing semi. Then the floor began to shake in earnest, and the pain in my throat subsided.

Teacups and ceramic pots rattled on the shelves. Then I heard a crash. Suddenly the pressure on my windpipe vanished, and I jerked upright with a gasp.

Dana was scrambling for the doorway, but then one of the shelves toppled over as the brick wall behind it began to crumble. A tidal wave of pots and cups and packets of tea tumbled down, and Dana's head disappeared.

Choking and coughing, I tried to get up, but the ground beneath me was shaking so badly that I couldn't get to my feet. I watched as a giant crack opened along the brick wall to my right, and I was hit by a mix of euphoria and relief.

A cloud of dust wafted up, and I choked. Then my muscles turned to jelly. My vision flickered, and I collapsed on the floor as the building broke apart around me. The last thing I saw was Desmond perched on a pile of rubble, his yellow eyes gleaming in the dark.

I CAME to with the wail of police sirens ringing in my ears and raindrops pattering on my upper lip. I could smell dirt and mortar and wet tea, and my mouth tasted like blood. My muscles ached as though I'd just been in a car wreck, and my teeth were chattering uncontrollably.

Low, hushed voices swirled around me, and a pair of strong arms lifted me out of the rubble. The feeling of rain became more pronounced, and I started to shiver. My savior's arms tightened around me, and I snuggled closer to a strong male chest that smelled like the forest in a rainstorm.

The world seemed to sway as my rescuer picked his way through the heap of crumbled brick. I heard the clink and crunch of ceramic underfoot, and the cool night air bit at my skin.

When I finally peeled my eyelids open, the street was awash in red and blue. The lights of first-responder vehicles were swirling all over the block, bouncing off the wet pavement and The Grand's stately facade.

All of a sudden, the urgency I'd felt in the tearoom all came rushing back. The murder. Dana. He was getting away!

I twisted my body to get back on my feet, and the arms around me tightened. "Whoa!"

Turning my head to the left, I saw the strong jaw of Officer Hamby, which was flecked with golden stubble.

"It was the teashop owner!" I gasped. "Dana Marzetti!"

"I know." Officer Hamby's voice was a low, angry rumble as he sat me down in the back of an ambulance. All at once, a team of medics swarmed me, and someone shined a penlight in my eyes.

"You *know*?" I choked, pushing the light away.

"We're booking him now," Hamby rumbled, nodding toward the farthest police cruiser, where Detective Pierce was putting Dana into the back of the cop car. The teashop owner's face was scratched and bruised, but he didn't look all that worse for the wear, considering a brick wall had fallen on him.

I gaped at Hamby and tried to pull my arm away before someone could put on a blood-pressure cuff. "But . . . *how*?"

The handsome lawman looked suddenly sheepish, and he nodded at the medics to give us a minute. Hamby shucked off his heavy police jacket, and I gaped at the thick tanned biceps straining at his black T-shirt. He draped the jacket around my shoulders, enveloping me in its warmth. It smelled heavenly — like pine trees and the forest floor — and I longed to take a deeper sniff.

"After you left the station, I couldn't shake the feeling that I should have heard you out. So I pulled a photo of Dana Marzetti off his website and had a buddy of mine at Interpol run it through the facial-recognition database. Turns out that Dana Marzetti is an alias." Hamby took a deep breath and dragged a hand through his hair. "Twenty years ago, he was Julian Dupris — a Canadian national wanted for poisoning a rival in Toronto. He's been flying under the radar ever since. When we got a call about a disturbance at the tearoom across from your hotel . . ." His lips tightened, and something like dread flickered over his face. "I got here as fast as I could."

I sucked in a breath and pulled Hamby's jacket more tightly around me.

"How did you know it was him?" he asked, those blue eyes boring into mine.

"I-I didn't . . . not at first. It was something my au—" I broke off. I couldn't mention my dead aunt, or Hamby would *really* think I was crazy. I shook my head. "Something someone said made me remember that strychnine comes from a tree that grows in Southern India. My gran and I had visited Dana's teashop, and I knew he'd been to India recently. Mathers planned to tear down the building where the teashop has been for decades. Dana's business would have been ruined."

A muscle in Hamby's jaw tightened. "You shouldn't have gone to confront him yourself."

"You wouldn't listen," I grumbled, glaring up at Hamby. "I almost got shot because —"

Suddenly it all came crashing back. The gun. The earthquake. Des.

"Desmond!" I croaked, jumping to my feet and swaying as all the blood rushed to my head. Desmond had been in the building when the back wall had come down. He'd probably been crushed to death. "I have to find my cat! He attacked Dana and saved my life, but he might be trapped —"

"Whoa. Take it easy," said Hamby, placing a warm hand on my shoulder and easing me back down. "Your cat is fine. He's over there." He nodded toward the huge fire engine, where Desmond was perched on the bumper. Two burly firefighters in bibs were huddled beside him, scratching his back as Des stretched regally.

My whole body seemed to crumple in relief, and hot tears sprang to my eyes. Desmond had saved my life back there. I'd have been shot if it weren't for him.

"What's this about your cat attacking the perp?" asked Hamby.

"H-he must have followed me into the building," I stammered, remembering how I'd left the back door cracked. It still didn't explain how Des had gotten out of the locked car, but I'd worry about that later. "Dana, he . . . He was holding a gun on me, and Des jumped down from a high shelf and made him drop the weapon."

Hamby's brows shot up, and he rubbed his neck wearily. "I don't suppose you can explain what you did to bring that wall down."

I shook my head, though a niggling realization was scratching at the back of my mind. I couldn't voice my theory without sounding like a lunatic, but I had the slightly uneasy feeling that I'd caused a mini earthquake.

Hamby stuffed his hands in his pockets and shrugged. "It was an old building. The foundation is in pretty bad shape. That wall was bound to fall down eventually. It's just lucky you weren't crushed."

I nodded, though I didn't think luck had much to do with it. When Dana had threatened me, I'd unleashed . . . *something*. The force behind the mini earthquake I'd felt had definitely come from me. That was why I felt as though I'd been run over by a train. I didn't have a scratch on me, apart from where I'd bit my own tongue.

Once Officer Hamby had finished with his line of questioning, the medics edged in to continue their examination. I sat still as they poked and prodded, turning the night's events over in my mind.

"Caroline!"

Gran's voice made me jerk my head around, earning a huff of irritation from the man who was trying to determine whether I'd suffered a concussion.

"Gran!" I called, jumping out of the ambulance and waving my arm to get her attention.

Gran had her "going out" shoes on and was wearing a

long gray coat over her sweatpants. She looked older and frailer than I'd ever seen her, but the moment she spotted me waving her over, all that worry seemed to evaporate.

"Oh, Caroline!" Gran made a beeline for the ambulance, gripping both my arms with a hard squeeze. "I was so worried. Why didn't you call? When they told me you'd been hurt —"

"I'm fine, Gran," I assured her, feeling terrible that she'd been so scared. "Really. But you shouldn't be here." I glanced down at her left ankle and lowered my voice. "You're under house arrest, remember?"

"Oh, that." Gran shook her head. "That handsome police officer called to tell me I could come over to make sure you were all right. He sounded so *concerned* for you." She waggled her eyebrows at me and then frowned. "What were you even *doing* here?"

I launched into the explanation of how I'd learned the identity of Jay Mathers's true killer, leaving out Aunt Lucille and the murder board we'd made. Gran's frown deepened when I told her about my breaking and entering, so when I got to the part about my confrontation with Dana, I decided to leave out the gun.

When I'd finished my story, she just shook her head. "I'm impressed that you figured out who killed Jay Mathers, but why didn't you just leave it up to the police?"

I opened my mouth to tell her I'd tried, but instead I just gave a shrug. "I'm tired, Gran. Let's get Desmond and go home."

CHAPTER TWENTY-FOUR

After my brush with death at the tearoom, I was glad to get back to Gran's. I peeled off my wet clothes, changed into a pair of pajamas, and curled up under one of her crocheted afghans with a cup of tea and some ginger cookies.

"I just can't *believe* it was Dana," Gran tutted, tucking her quilted robe more tightly around her and settling into a wingback chair. Snowball was snoozing hard on his bed by her chair, and Desmond was snuggled into the crook of my legs.

After I'd finally told Gran how Des had saved my life, she'd seemed to regard the cat with new appreciation. She'd opened a can of tuna for his dinner, given him some pets, and even relaxed her no-cats-on-the-furniture rule for the night.

"All these years that I've gone to that tearoom, and because of him I almost went to prison for murder!" She shook her head in disgust. "And the poison was in the *air conditioning*?"

"Yep. Dana must have sneaked in when Mathers's assistant left to get his coffee and placed the poison in the window unit."

Gran looked amazed. "That's why my cookies tested positive for the poison."

I nodded. "There was so much dust from the construction at the office that the police didn't think anything of the little bit of powder left on Mathers's desk. If you'd still been there when the air conditioning had kicked on . . ." I shuddered at the thought.

Gran just shook her head.

"There's still one thing I haven't figured out," I said, turning to look at her and narrowing my eyes. "What *were* you doing at Mathers's office the morning he was killed?"

"I told you," said Gran in an exasperated tone. "I went over there to gloat. That man thought he was going to steal The Mountain Shadow Grand right out from under your Aunt Lucille's dead body, so I brought some cookies to offer my condolences."

I squinted at her. "Nice try. But I don't believe for one second that you'd have brought cookies if you'd gone there to gloat."

Gran pressed her lips together and shrugged, but she wouldn't meet my gaze.

"Gran . . ."

"Oh, all right!" she grumbled. "My goodness, you're pushy!" She rolled her eyes, fidgeted in her chair, and loosed an enormous sigh. "If you must know, Jay Mathers was — and had been for a long time — sniffing around my car."

I raised a disbelieving eyebrow. "Come again?"

"The Pinto is in really good condition for its age, you

know, and they don't make them anymore. It's sort of a . . . collector's item." She waved a hand. "I'll bet you Jay Mathers had come by the house at least fifteen times over the years trying to buy that old car."

"So why didn't you sell it? I thought you didn't drive anymore."

"I might not be able to drive, Caroline, but it's still my car!" She let out an irritable huff. "This may seem silly to you, but your grandfather and I got that car brand new in nineteen seventy-nine. I only drove it a few times a week, so it doesn't have that many miles on it. It was the last car he and I bought together, and I feel a little sentimental about it."

I opened my mouth to say something — what, I didn't know — but Gran cut me off. "It's silly that I've held on to it all this time. I sort of hoped someone *would* steal it so I wouldn't have to get rid of it myself. But I decided that if I was going to sell it, I'd let it go to a good cause." She cracked a wry grin. "It would have given me great pleasure to use the sale to stick it to ol' Jay Mathers. I'd planned on offering to sell it for twenty thousand and then turn around and use the cash to pay back the taxes on the property he was so eager to pounce on."

"Gran . . ." I raised an eyebrow. "That's diabolical."

"Well, he wanted the car so badly I figured he'd be willing to overpay. He might have caught on to my scheme, because he basically told me to take a hike, even after I brought him the cookies."

I let out a breath and shook my head. Gran was really something else.

"Well, you don't have to get rid of the Pinto on my account," I said. "I'm selling the hotel."

Gran looked suddenly angry. "Now, why would you go and do a thing like that?"

"Because . . ." I took a deep breath. I knew I needed to talk to Gran about her finances, but it wasn't a conversation I was looking forward to having. "I can't afford to pay the back taxes on the property, and . . . neither can you."

"Who told you that?"

I fixed her with a hard look. "Come on, Gran. I think we just need to let the hotel go."

"Caroline, if there's something you aren't telling me—"

"Officer Hamby pulled your financial records," I said in a rush. "He told me you used the settlement from the railroad to pay back a loan you and Gramps had taken out on the house. You've used up a lot of his life-insurance money already, and all you have besides that is social security."

Gran's wiry gray eyebrows drew together. "Now, I'm not sure why that handsome busybody was digging into my personal finances, but he doesn't know what he's talking about."

I frowned. "He doesn't?"

"Well, he's right about your grandfather's settlement. I did use it to pay off the loan, but I'm not hurting by any means."

"You're not?"

"Of course not. Your grandfather and I didn't have a lot of investments, but we did manage to hold on to the farm, you know."

Ah, the infamous farm.

Gran fixed me with a patronizing look. "I don't know if you realize this, Caroline, but the cost of farmland in

Kansas has gotten quite dear. When I first learned of Lucille's wish for the hotel, I was angry. But then I got to thinking that it could be a good investment for you."

I raised my eyebrows.

"So I went and put an ad out for the farm."

"You're *selling*?" I spluttered. "Gran, you can't sell the farm! Not on my account."

"Oh, keep your shirt on." Gran rolled her eyes. "I'm not *selling* the farm, honey. I'm leasing it."

"*Leasing* it? Like, to farm on?"

Gran nodded, a slight smile playing on her lips. "I already found a very nice tenant. He signed the lease this morning, and I got R.P.'s assistant to go by the treasurer's office and pay the property taxes on the hotel."

My mouth fell open. All this time I'd been working on the case, I'd had no idea what Gran had been up to. "Gran . . . you should have kept the money."

"What for? The house is paid for, and I have all the clothes I'll ever need. Snowball doesn't eat but one tiny bag of LuckyChow every two weeks. So long as the price of Vienna sausages doesn't go through the roof, he and I are all set."

I shook my head in disbelief, flabbergasted that Gran had managed to lease the farm and repay the back taxes while under house arrest.

"Anyway . . . it's about time the farm started paying for itself," she mused. "It's where I grew up — and it kept us fed — but it's been the source of a lot of heartache over the last few years."

"Because Aunt Lucille loaned against it to buy the hotel, and you and Gramps had to bail her out?"

Gran looked startled by my revelation. "Who told you about that?"

"Uh . . ." For a moment, I considered telling her about Aunt Lucille's ghost, but I figured she'd been through enough for one day.

"I suppose it doesn't matter. Yes, your aunt Lucille got in over her head on that deal, and your grandfather and I had to make a choice: Either we could let the farm go, or we could buy her out." Gran looked suddenly melancholy. "We decided to buy her out, but to do that, we had to open a line of credit on the house. It wasn't more than we could manage, but it meant your grandfather had to put off his retirement." She sighed. "He was on his way to work one day when he was hit by that train. The signal was malfunctioning, and I suppose he took that route so often that he didn't bother to look both ways." She shook her head. "It was wrong of me, but I blamed Lucille for his death. If she hadn't taken a gamble on that hotel, your grandfather would have been home with me rather than on his way to work."

Suddenly, it all made sense. Gran hadn't been angry with her sister because she'd put them in bad financial straits. A part of her had blamed Lucille for Gramps's death.

"Maybe I shouldn't have been so hard on her," Gran mused. "Lucille was never the careful sort. When she saw something she wanted, she just went for it. There was no talking her out of it."

"Like her singing and acting career?"

Gran chuckled. "Yes. Lucille was incorrigible. My parents about had kittens when she told them she'd bought a train ticket and was going west."

"You never told me you and Lucille had a two-woman act at The Grand, you know."

Gran turned her head to look at me, her face as white as a sheet. "Where on *earth* did you hear that?"

I opened my mouth without having any idea what I was going to say. I couldn't exactly tell her that Aunt Lucille's ghost had told me about Gran's brief stint on the stage.

"That is a story I planned to take to my grave, young lady," said Gran in a stern voice. "I don't even think your grandfather knew about that! I certainly didn't tell my parents."

Bracing herself on the arms of her chair, Gran lifted herself out of her seat and toddled over to the bookshelf. Several old photo albums were crowded along the bottom row, and she returned with a small leather-bound album.

"I'm sure I have a picture in here somewhere," she mused, flipping through the old black-and-white photographs. There were pictures of Gramps in his navy uniform, photos of the two of them together, and photos of people I didn't recognize.

"Oh. Here." A faint smile tugged at the corners of Gran's mouth as she tapped a fingernail on the photograph. I leaned over for a better look at the crumpled, slightly blurry picture.

The photo showed her and Aunt Lucille dressed in what I could only describe as Vegas showgirl getups. They wore their hair down in long ringlets with giant feathers sticking up in the back. Their legs were bare apart from their fishnet stockings, and they wore matching T-strap heels.

"We were so young," Gran mused, pressing her wrinkled fingertips reverently to the photo.

Lucille didn't look that much different from her ghost, though Gran couldn't have been a day over seventeen — her face plump and unlined. Lucille wore the coy look of a young woman used to parading in front of an audience. Gran's face was turned up toward her big sister, a shy smile playing on her lips.

Gran chewed on her bottom lip, and then she sighed and shook her head. "That was a long time ago."

"Some things haven't changed," I said, thinking of Lucille. She was still that vivacious young woman at heart, and in a way, so was Gran.

"Is that so?" Gran chuckled and wiped a stray tear from under her eye. "I don't think I could cancan these days if my life depended on it."

"You mean, you can-*can't*?" I laughed at my own bad joke and shrugged. "The hotel is more or less the same, and it's over a hundred years old."

Gran gave me a wry look. "As someone who is ninety-two percent of a hundred years old, I can promise you that that's not true."

I waved this away. "Hotels and grandmothers are like fine wine."

"Expensive?"

"They just get better with age."

"Uh-huh." Gran snapped the photo album shut and set it aside before heaving herself out of her chair. "Tell that to my darn knees."

As Gran stood, Snowball lifted his head.

"Come on, Snow. We'd better get some sleep. It's been a long day, and we have a lot of work to do if we want to save Lucille's hotel."

CHAPTER TWENTY-FIVE

The next morning, I had a bid from the contractor Miles Briggs waiting for me in my inbox. When I saw the amount, Gran's "protein shake" spurted out of my nose, showering my keyboard in chocolate milk. I coughed and pounded my chest with a fist, trying to clear my airways.

"What's wrong?" Gran huffed from the living room, punching her fists in time with her Tae Bo video.

"Oh, nothing," I sighed. "Just got a quote back from the contractor."

"Well, there's always money in the Pinto if we need to sell it."

"I'm afraid this isn't Pinto kind of money, Gran. It's not even Porsche money."

"I've got some Precious Moments figurines in the attic you could sell on eBay if you're a little short."

"Mmm, I'm not sure that'll cover it."

Gran shrugged and turned her attention back to Billy

Blanks as I massaged my eyeballs. Aunt Lucille's memorial service was on Monday, and I needed caffeine if I was going to work up the motivation to put together her "celebration of life" slide show and make some calls to other contractors.

Slamming my planner shut, I scooped my pens and highlighters into my purse and headed out the front door. Desmond skittered out after me with a *yee-ow*, and I opened the passenger door of Gran's car so he could hop in. Since I'd inherited Des, I'd sort of gotten used to having him tag along as my personal sidekick. And after he'd saved my life back at the teashop, I couldn't deny he was useful.

He stayed in the car as I got out in front of Déjà Brew and followed the sweet scent of espresso up the sidewalk. I tugged open the front door and took a step inside — nearly colliding with Officer Hamby. He was carrying an extra-large coffee in each hand and a paper sack tucked under one arm.

His eyes went wide when he saw me, and he jerked back to avoid a collision — sloshing coffee all down his front.

"I'm sorry!" I wailed, still standing in the open doorway.

"Don't apologize," Hamby chuckled, backing into the coffee shop. "I was in too big a hurry."

Face beet red, I slid around him to grab a fistful of napkins from the station by the entrance. I started to blot the stain on his uniform but stopped when I realized how awkward it was to be patting the detective's chest.

I cleared my throat and tried to give him the napkins before realizing that his hands were full. Hamby backed up to set the drinks on a nearby table so he could attend to his shirt.

A loud snort caught my attention, and I turned in the direction of the noise. Amber had been watching our stilted dance from behind the counter and was positively rolling with laughter.

"Sorry about your shirt," I mumbled, grimacing at the huge dark stain down the front of Hamby's uniform.

"It's fine," he said. "I have five more just like it."

He stopped dabbing at the stain and looked up at me with those dazzling blue eyes. My breath hitched as I caught his gaze, and I remembered how delicious he'd smelled when he'd carried me out of the wreckage. "I'm glad I bumped into you, actually," he said. "I . . . thought about coming by your gran's place this morning, but I figured I wouldn't be welcome."

"That depends," I said, flushing with pleasure and folding my hands behind my back.

"On?"

"On whether you have any pull over at the Department of Motor Vehicles."

Officer Hamby frowned in confusion.

"Gran had her license revoked a while ago," I explained. "Maybe you could help her get it reinstated?"

"Oh." Hamby laughed, and I noticed the cute way the corners of his eyes crinkled when he smiled. "I'll look into it."

I swallowed and nodded, my stomach doing all kinds of nervous backflips. "What, uh . . ." I cleared my throat. "What did you want to see me about, officer?"

"Call me Will."

"Will." His name was like chocolate on my tongue, and it was all I could do to keep from repeating it.

A grin twitched at the corner of his mouth. "I owe you an apology."

My eyebrows shot up. I hadn't expected *that*.

"I was dismissive of your theory when you came into the station," he said, sucking in a heavy breath and squinting at a spot just over my shoulder. "I should have taken the time to listen."

"Oh." I looked down at my shoes and back at Hamby — Will — feeling a little smug.

"That's not to say you should have gone barging into that tearoom," he added in a stern voice. "You could have been killed, and I still don't entirely believe the story about your cat."

"His name is Desmond, and he's very protective of me."

"Be that as it may . . . I don't know if I could have lived with myself if something had happened to you because I didn't take the time to listen."

At those words, the butterflies in my stomach felt as though they were doing backflips off a high dive. "It's not *me* you have to apologize to."

"Oh, no?" Will looked concerned.

I shook my head. "Now that Gran knows what that old rat poison is good for, she might incorporate it into her cookie recipe for policemen she doesn't like."

Will let out a hard bark of laughter that gave me an unexpected thrill. "Well, it's a good thing they haven't released the poison from evidence." He braced a hand against the door jamb behind me, eyes twinkling as he looked down at me. "Give me a chance to make it up to you?"

I nodded wordlessly, too breathless to speak. Why did I get the feeling that Officer Will was flirting with me?

For a moment, the two of us just stood there, and I found myself leaning in. But then he pushed himself off the doorjamb, picked up his coffees, and started backing out of the door. "Take it easy, Caroline."

My heart was still a little bouncy from my conversation with Will as I keyed into The Grand. Desmond slinked between my legs as I surveyed the lobby and inhaled the old, antique smell of the place.

The Mountain Shadow Grand was really mine. Mine to own. Mine to fix. Mine to get up and running again. I still didn't have any idea how I was going to fund the hotel's renovations. Now that I was out of a job, I couldn't even fund my *life*.

It was a slightly terrifying prospect, but on the other hand, not having a job simplified things. It freed up my time to focus on The Grand, and it wasn't as though I would have been able to manage the renovations from Chicago anyway. If I found a subletter and moved out of my expensive West Loop apartment, I could make two months' severance last a lot longer.

Even though I was adrift, the idea of staying in Mountain Shadow gave me a little thrill. I wasn't really sure if I could make a go of it as a hotel proprietress, but it was an exciting prospect. I had entire lists of the to-do lists I needed to make bouncing around in my head, but first I needed to see —

"Caroline! There you are!" The disembodied voice seemed to boom out of nowhere, making my heart jump.

I whirled around, hand clasped to my chest, and came face to face with Aunt Lucille. Her long jet curls were pinned atop her head, and she was dressed in a long silken nightgown with a matching robe edged in lace. She held a steaming china cup clutched in her manicured fingers, and I could have sworn I could smell her coffee.

"Aunt Lucille," I gasped, trying to calm my racing heart. "Don't sneak up on me like that! You scared me half to death."

"Scared *you*? Young lady, I have been worried sick! You ran off last night with this grand theory about the owner of the tearoom. The next thing I know, there's a loud rumble across the street and police crawling all over the place!" Aunt Lucille blinked those impossibly long fake eyelashes of hers, which she seemed to wear at every hour of the day. "Oh, I was afraid that terrible man had done something awful to you. I didn't sleep a wink!"

"I'm sorry I didn't fill you in sooner, but — hang on. Ghosts *sleep*?"

"In a manner of speaking, yes." Lucille sounded haughty at first. Then she looked confused. "At least, I think I do. Certainly I go someplace else and . . . have a little rest." She trailed off on the last few words, sounding less certain than she had initially.

Maybe ghosts didn't actually sleep, but whatever remained of one's spirit after death couldn't materialize every hour of the day. Maybe after a while, it just went out — sort of like a burned-out lightbulb.

"I'm sorry that you were worried about me," I said gently. "I would have come by last night, but Gran was pretty shaken up herself."

"Yes, I expect she would be," said Lucille, sounding a little faint. "Come up to my room, and we'll have a chat. I want to hear *everything* — every last detail — but I think I might need a little splash of brandy."

I was dying to ask Aunt Lucille about her seemingly bottomless supply of cigarettes, fine clothes, and — apparently — brandy but decided to refrain. It didn't seem polite to ask, and she'd been so unsettled after I'd asked about her sleep habits.

Once we were settled in Aunt Lucille's preferred suite on the fourth floor and she'd procured a bottle of Cusenier cherry brandy seemingly out of thin air, I launched into the story of how I'd broken into the tearoom to investigate Dana, only to be caught snooping. When I finished, Aunt Lucille was curled at the foot of the bed in her long silken nightdress, her knees drawn up under her chin and her thin arms clasped around her shins.

"Oh, my dear. That is just *terrifying*. If I weren't already dead, you'd have given me a coronary with that story." She reached down to stroke Desmond, who was sprawled on the bed beside his former mistress. Her fingers didn't make any tracks in his glossy black fur, but he closed his eyes and purred as if he really could feel her touch. "*Bravo*, Des. You're a hero."

"He is," I admitted. "If he hadn't shown up when he did, I might be haunting the tearoom right now."

Aunt Lucille let out a shuddering gasp. "Don't you even *joke* about that! Just thinking of you in such peril . . .

and me right across the street, unable to do anything about it!"

The memory of those horrifying moments in the storeroom still left me cold, but not because I'd been held at gunpoint. So far I hadn't told anyone about what I'd experienced in the tearoom — that explosive feeling of power and relief just as the wall came down.

I knew it was probably just the adrenaline. There were all sorts of stories of people experiencing visions and other so-called "miracles" during a near-death experience, and yet I couldn't seem to get it out of my head.

I was on the verge of asking Aunt Lucille about it when another question popped into my head. "Wait . . . Are you saying you can't leave the hotel?"

As soon as the words left my mouth, I wished I could stuff them back in. It was probably a horrible thing to ask, given that she already seemed to be trapped between this world and the next.

"Alas, I cannot," said Aunt Lucille with a wistful sigh. "I have tried, believe me, but it seems that my spirit is tied to this hotel."

I sucked in a breath as the implication of that statement hit me. "So if Jay Mathers had succeeded in his plan to demolish the hotel . . ."

"It would be curtains for me. Or perhaps I'd be doomed to wander this site from here until eternity . . ." She trailed off in a dramatic fashion and then waved her hand. "Or something."

"This is all so strange," I murmured, staring at Aunt Lucille sitting there with the sunlight casting off her silk gown. She seemed so real — so solid — and yet . . .

"I must be losing my mind," I muttered. "First I'm seeing spirits, and then —"

Aunt Lucille turned her elegant head to look at me. "And then what, dear?"

I swallowed, wishing I'd just kept my mouth shut. I knew it was crazy, but it wasn't as though Aunt Lucille could come back from the dead and have me committed. She was probably the safest person to tell.

I took a deep breath. "Last night, when Dana had me trapped in the tearoom, I was so . . . *angry*. Angry at my ex-fiancé . . . angry at Officer Will for not listening . . . angry at myself for not making him listen. When I released that anger, I . . ." I trailed off, shaking my head. "This is going to sound crazy, but I could have *sworn* that I brought that wall down on Dana."

For a moment, the words just hung in the air between us. I'd expected Aunt Lucille to jump in to say I was being silly — or that it was just an accident. Instead, the corner of her mouth lifted in a coy smile that raised the hairs along the back of my neck.

"But that's *impossible*," I added. "Right?"

And here I was talking to a ghost. I'd *definitely* lost my mind.

"For most people, yes. I agree it would be impossible. But for a Blackthorne . . ." Aunt Lucille trailed off in a way I found extremely disconcerting.

"Aunt Lucille." I gave her a stern look. "What are you trying to say?"

"Just that the Blackthornes are, and have always been, endowed with certain — eh, *gifts*?"

I stared her down. "What kind of gifts?"

"Gifts of the paranormal variety. Communing with the

spirits . . . telepathy . . . otherworldly perception. I myself was plagued by the most disturbing dreams in life, though those seem to have ceased now that I've left my body."

I frowned. "Are you trying to tell me that people in our family have supernatural powers?"

"Not everyone," Lucille conceded. "Your great-grandfather — my father — had powers of precognition, though they never manifested as dreams. Your grandmother never had any such inclinations. She was certainly not subject to the night terrors *I* had as a child. I used to wake up screaming night after night in the grip of cold fear. I was completely inconsolable, and it would keep me from sleeping for days at a time. The most terrifying part was that most of what I dreamt actually came true."

"Like what?"

Aunt Lucille's face went dark. "One night, I dreamt of the most horrific explosion. There was dust everywhere. I couldn't see a thing, except for the face of our farmhand, Chip. Chip was in excruciating pain, but I couldn't do anything to help him. I tried to tell my parents, but they assumed I was just a child having a nightmare."

"So what happened?"

"Three days later, the boiler blew on the threshing machine, and Chip lost his leg."

For a moment, I just stared. "Aunt Lucille, that could have just been a coincidence."

"Yes." Lucille nodded. "Yes, it could have. So could the dream I had about our cat being attacked by coyotes or the barn fire that almost killed my father. But after a time, there were simply too many 'coincidences.' I knew I had to get away from the farm, but I could never outrun the dreams — no matter how far I went. I tried everything. Gin. Nerve pills. Hypnosis. Nothing worked. Eventually I decided that if I could not banish the dreams, I needed to understand them. So I became a student of the occult and began to develop my abilities. That's what led me back to Mountain Shadow after my time in Hollywood."

"Mountain Shadow?"

Lucille smiled. "This town has its own magic. Have you ever been able to commune with spirits before you came to Colorado?"

"Well . . . no," I stammered, reluctant to admit that I was "communing with spirits." It sounded *way* too woo-woo. "You think I developed my ability to see dead people when I came to Mountain Shadow?"

"How else do you explain the fact that we're able to speak to one another now?" Lucille chuckled. "No one else can see me, Caroline. Just you. I've tested it."

"You *tested* it?"

Lucille nodded. "I flashed that contractor, Mr. Briggs. Poor fellow didn't see a thing."

I snorted, unable to get the image of ghost Lucille flashing my contractor out of my mind. "He must not have. Otherwise, he might have given me a better price on the renovations."

"How much does he want?"

I raised my eyebrows. "Let's just say that I thought he'd made a mistake and put one too many zeroes behind it. I'm going to get another quote, but I don't know how Gran and I are going to come up with the money to renovate this place."

"Oh, pish-posh." Lucille waved this away and got to her feet, sauntering out of the room and down the hall toward the elevator. "We'll find the money, dear. You just leave it to me."

I wasn't sure where Lucille was headed, but I followed her down the hallway. I needed to get back to Gran's and start making some phone calls.

"Money is not the real problem, you know," said Lucille once I'd joined her in the elevator.

"Oh no?"

She shook her head. "The real trouble will be convincing the more *perturbed* resident spirits that our venture is worthwhile."

I raised my eyebrows. "There is *so much* to unpack in that sentence." When I'd inherited the hotel, I'd been unaware that The Grand had "resident spirits" at all.

"Well, you know, most of them are not as young as I," said Lucille, putting a delicate hand to her chest. "I'm afraid many of them have become rather set in their ways."

"You were ninety-eight when you died," I reminded her, sliding the cage door shut and punching the button for the first floor.

"But I'm still *twenty*-eight at heart, dear — and an entrepreneur. These dusty old ghosts have grown rather tiresome. They aren't at *all* happy with the proposed changes."

As the inner cage door slid shut on its own, I turned to look at Lucille. "Is that . . . going to be a problem?"

"Oh, no. No, no, no. At least, I don't think so. I'm sure they'll come aro—"

Just then, the elevator gave a stomach-churning lurch, and it felt as though the floor had dropped out from under me. Bertha shot down through the shaft as though someone had cut the cable, and I had to throw out an arm to keep from crashing into the door.

I bent my knees, bracing for the inevitable crash, but then the pulley system seemed to re-engage, and Bertha abruptly slowed her descent. The sudden change in momentum caused me to stumble, and I hit the floor on one knee.

The elevator dinged as we reached the ground level, and the inner cage door opened automatically. Weak daylight was filtering into the lobby through the gaps around the plywood, and I could hear birds chirping merrily outside as if nothing was amiss.

Gasping and shaking, I pulled myself up and tore open the outer cage door.

Never again, I told myself fervently. I would take the stairs.

But as I staggered out into the lobby, something flickered in my periphery. I glanced toward the broken grandfather clock, and in the ribbons of golden-white light shining through the cracks in the plywood, I could have sworn I saw a sallow-skinned man dressed in coveralls and a tattered cap.

The man was skin and bones beneath his clothing, and a tool belt hung from his narrow hips. He met my gaze for the briefest moment before vanishing in a swirl of dust.

I turned back around to face Aunt Lucille, who was braced against the elevator, clutching her chest. "You were *saying?*"

AUTHOR'S NOTE

Thank you for reading *Better Off Dead*. I hope you enjoyed the story. If this is your first experience reading one of my books, welcome. We have fun here in Mountain Shadow. If you're a long-time fan, thank you for taking a chance on a brand-new series. Your support means the world to me.

As I was wrapping up my Witches of Mountain Shadow series, I knew I wasn't done with that world. I was still so in love with the town and many of the characters who live there — as well as Mountain Shadow's special brand of magic. Readers have been asking me for a true spin-off to the series with Emry and Sloan, but I wasn't ready to write that just yet.

I knew I wanted a fresh start with some brand-new characters, and Caroline and Gran came to me almost immediately. I also had an idea for a haunted hotel that I really wanted to play with. I'm completely obsessed with historic hotels — especially if they happen to be haunted. Fans of Witches of Mountain Shadow will know that the town is *very* loosely based on Manitou Springs, Colorado,

AUTHOR'S NOTE

and The Mountain Shadow Grand is also an amalgamation of a few real-life places.

Last summer, I stumbled upon the condemned Hotel St. Cloud in Cañon City, Colorado, which has a fascinating history. It was originally built in Silver Cliff in the late eighteen hundreds and was only accessible by stage coach. It was considered a very swanky hotel in its day with steam heat, running water, electric lights, and private baths.

When mining in the area slowed and ore mills shut down, the owners deconstructed the Hotel St. Cloud and moved it, brick by brick, to Cañon City. It was during the reconstruction that the fourth floor was added. The hotel weathered the Great Depression (only closing its dining room) and hosted film crews and movie stars such as Burt Lancaster and Robert Walker.

Despite its storied history, the Hotel St. Cloud has had more than its fair share of financial woes. In fact, the move to Cañon City was delayed by the county treasurer for unpaid taxes. The Hotel St. Cloud shuttered its doors for the first time in 1989 and has changed hands (and names) so frequently that I can't help wondering if the place is cursed. Still, grant money has poured into the project of restoring the hotel, and it's slated to reopen in 2024.

Not long after I saw the Hotel St. Cloud for the first time, I read a newspaper article saying that the historic Victor Hotel had been revived. When I stepped in one day to take a peek, I was told that it still had a functioning birdcage elevator (which was supposed to be haunted, of course). The elevator was out of order at the time of my visit, since some "hooligans" had been jumping in the elevator on Halloween.

AUTHOR'S NOTE

It felt weird to hang out at the Victor Hotel when I wasn't staying there, so I paid a visit to the Pioneers Museum in Colorado Springs to see its birdcage elevator. I rode that elevator many times and even worked on the scene with Rusty while I was at the museum to really capture Bertha's "essence."

A few early readers have asked me if Gran is based off a real person. While I definitely took some inspiration from my own granny (who is ninety-six at the time of this writing), Virginia McCrithers is definitely her own person. While my granny *does* share Gran's special brand of humor and drink chocolate milk for breakfast, she doesn't wear tracksuits or work out to Billy Blanks. (To my knowledge, none of Granny's sisters were burlesque dancers, but they did grow up on a farm during the Great Depression.)

I had a blast imagining how Gran might interact with some of Mountain Shadow's established residents, and I got a kick out of having Caroline meet old favorites like Bellamy and Wesley (Detective Pierce). If you are a fan of Witches of Mountain Shadow, you won't want to miss the upcoming books where Caroline meets Jinx and Daphne.

My favorite part of writing *Better Off Dead* was writing the relationships between Gran, Caroline, and Aunt Lucille. I think there's often a generational divide in families and that we don't spend enough time tapping into the wisdom and experience of the oldest people we know. Maybe this is why those in their eighties and nineties are conspicuously missing from most books, movies, and TV shows — except sometimes as comic relief.

At a certain age, characters get reduced to "the old granny" who might be hard of hearing or say cringeworthy things at the dinner table. They're seldom

AUTHOR'S NOTE

portrayed as three-dimensional people who are still actively working through their core wounds and taking on new challenges. They're often shielded from the real drama going on in younger people's lives, even though they've lived the *most* life, and there's probably nothing one could tell someone in their nineties that would be very shocking.

I feel lucky that I've gotten to know my granny as an adult and hear her perspective and advice as I raise my son. (It helps when your grandma is a feisty one who will give it to you straight.) I would certainly love to solve murder mysteries with her if I ever got the chance.

If you enjoyed this story, be sure to sign up for my newsletter at www.tarahbenner.com so you never miss a new Mountain Shadow Mystery.

Until next time, happy reading!

THERE ARE MORE MYSTERIES
TO SOLVE!

Find your next great read at
www.tarahbenner.com.
Watch on YouTube @TarahBennerAuthor.
"Like" the books on Facebook.

Printed in Great Britain
by Amazon